Janusz Anderman

THE EDGE OF THE WORLD

Preface by Jerzy Pilch

translated by Nina Taylor

readers international

The title of this book in Polish is *Kraj swiata*, first published in Polish by Institut Littéraire, Maisons-Laffitte, France, 1988. © Janusz Anderman, 1988. The story ''Jakoś pusto'' appeared in PULS 24 (Winter 1984-85), London. © PULS Publications, 1985. This story appeared under the title ''Postscript 1985: Empty...Sort of'' in Janusz Anderman's first book in English, *Poland Under Black Light* (Readers International, 1985), English translation © Readers International, 1985.

First published in English by Readers International, Inc., USA, and Readers International, London. Editorial inquiries to London office at 8 Strathray Gardens, London NW3 4NY, England. US/Canadian inquiries to Subscriber Service Department, P.O. Box 959, Columbia, Louisiana 71418-0959 USA.

Cover art: ''Mask'' by Stasys Eidrigevicius, Warsaw
Cover design by Jan Brychta
Typeset by Grassroots Typeset, London N3
Printed and bound in Great Britain by Richard Clay Ltd., Bungay, Suffolk

Library of Congress Catalog Card Number: 88-061402

British Library Cataloguing in Publication Data
Anderman, Janusz, *1949-*
    The edge of the world.
    I. Title II. Kraj swiata. *English*
    891.8'537 [F]

ISBN 0-930523-49-0 hardcover
ISBN 0-930523-50-4 paperback

About the translator: Nina Taylor studied Russian at Oxford, and Polish at the School of Slavonic and East European Studies in London. She specializes in 19th and 20th century Polish Literature.

CONTENTS

Preface

The 'audibility' of Janusz Anderman's prose was noted in his first two books, *Dead Telephone Games* (Warsaw, 1976) and *Playing for Time* (Warsaw, 1979). Indeed, the tag 'linguistic ear' appears to have stuck to Anderman for good and all. It was apparent, albeit less ostentatiously, in his third book, *Poland Under Black Light*, which has not been published in Poland but has appeared in Polish and English abroad.

In *The Edge of the World*, his second collection of stories to be translated into English, this 'audibility' assumes a new creative twist in the dialogues of his characters, their weird ripostes and aphorisms, and in the poetic, if fragmentary, descriptions. Yet, while the writer's ear faithfully registers street talk, one cannot help observing that he now commands a greater range of grotesque devices: his caricature of overheard Polish is more pronounced, and his vision of reality more extreme, than in his earlier work.

This style and subject matter derive from wider issues. For in the years between the publication of the first two books in Poland and this new book abroad, the world — our 'country at the edge of the world' in particular — has undergone not a few distortions and contortions. Yet can one argue that the Polish reality of the 1970s presented in *Playing for Time* was less grotesque than the Polish reality of the 1980s presented in *The Edge of the World* ? The reverse may equally well be true. Were the 1950s more grotesque than the 1980s? What was it really like then, in the days of Bierut or in Gomulka's time? 'Grandpa,' a ten-year-old boy asks in "Poland Still?"', 'say Grandpa, what was it like in Walesa's time?' 'In Walesa's time, to be perfectly honest — the old man strains his eyes — to tell you the truth it wasn't that simple. There's more than one way. It varied like. One way and the other. That's what. Something like.' Anderman doubtless knows that this is no answer to the boy's question. At the same time he seems to be saying that only a child can insist on an answer — or at least a fundamental and comprehensive answer — to 'what was it like in Walesa's time?' Only fragmentary answers are available. One might say for instance that in Walesa's day, and after, Polish life began to abound in picturesque collective scenes not encountered in such intensity before.

The 1980s may or may not be more grotesque than the previous decades. But one thing is evident on the landscape: the spectacle of large heterogeneous groups of people. Apart from gatherings immemorial, like shop queues and May Day parades (the balloon with the slogan 'Warm Welcome to the Congress' in the story "The Three Kings" has been 'parading past the tribune for years. At the head, in the middle, a sort of symbol like. In Gierek's day, too, only it went a different route, maybe you remember…'), new throngs have sprung up, more distinctly provoked by presentday events: some more or less purposeful demonstrations, more or less nonsensical chains of pure hearts, phenomena that have undoubtedly provided the inspiration for Anderman's book, and — one could even say — have become central to it.

Obvious as it may seem, this thesis must be qualified. Firstly, it is worth noting that *Playing for Time* and *Dead*

Telephone Games are also 'books about the crowd', both being based on a peculiar kind of polyphony, their texture woven from a series of monologues, dialogues, utterances, the voices of chance passersby, workmen, artists, taxi drivers and madmen. *The Edge of the World* is thus the sequel to Anderman's previous books, whose narrator paced through the spectral urban landscape, recording random 'voices of poor folk'. Nowadays his task is easier because the voices are to be heard often enough in the same place.

Secondly, the crowd in *The Edge of the World* has similarities to characters in the puppet theatre. The eye and ear of the ubiquitous narrator time and again catch the characters (or sketches of characters): the Journalist, the Provocateur, the Official, the Drunkard, the Patriot Pole, the Oppositionist Pole, the Idiot Pole. They declaim convulsively on some current issue and vanish again into the crowd.

Their language and the issues on which they pronounce are, of course, not that of the puppet theatre. Their speech is incomprehensible pulp-speak, 'rustling like dry ivy'. They make incredible calculations, ejaculate scraps of crazy arguments and declarations, tell about uncommon rituals, quote sermons, TV programs and press communiqués, relate the history of miracles and their own obsessions, attempt to stammer out some generalized truth about shop deliveries or Walesa. But add to this style of speech their convulsive gesticulations (paroxysms of insane laughter, shaking of fists, jerking of heads) and their grotesque costumes, and one senses again the puppet theatre.

The whirlpool of language is so swift that the need to emphasize individual issues, distinguish voices, and distribute miniature roles occasionally calls for purely external devices. Hence the rich panoply of headgear — church guards' helmets, caps with tassels, white militia caps, berets, pointed newspaper hats, cyclists' caps — with which Anderman's crowd is bedecked.

The Edge of the World, in short, offers a vision that embraces everything, from an argument about a cockroach to dialogues about Poland, from the fire at the National Theatre to the 'living photograph', and this vision is sufficiently grotesque to be apocalyptic.

Indeed, the only act in the entire book that is not grotesque, but is natural, positive and (I apologize for the pathos) victorious, is the act of silence. In "Empty...Sort of" two writers summoned for police interrogation remain silent. And their silence, lasting many hours, brings a deeper metaphysical meaning. To paraphrase the Western woman reporter (in "Poland Still?") attempting to formulate the essence of the event: Silence is victory.

The conversation between two writers, which frames the book, is also concerned with silence (in this case, defeat). Struck for a variety of reasons with creative impotence, the two writers debate some of the consequences of 'living in interesting times'. The totality of our 'interesting times' strikes them as a panopticon, a grotesque apocalypse, as pulp-speak. They also realize that the question 'what was it like in Walesa's time' cannot be answered for the time being, that only a partial, fragmentary answer can be given, exemplified by individual instances such as the negro Zmijewski or the taxi driver-mathematician. There is no guarantee, however, that individual cases will shed light on the universal obscurity.

The writers are treated seriously by Anderman (at least, I think they are), they speak articulately and are endowed with a deep and bitter awareness of the present hour. Yet they are no different from the rest of the characters populating the pages of *The Edge of the World*. Nothing distinguishes them from the crowd. Or rather, nothing distinguishes the crowd from them. For the crowd also attempts to articulate some manner of truth, to escape from paralysis, to decipher at least a fragment of the new epic silence weighing upon it. This is the basis of the comedy, as well as the tragedy, in the dialogues, monologues and utterances staged by Anderman: the concrete situation in which an ordinary consumer of hotdogs finds himself contrasts with the narrator's omniscience regarding the grotesque overall picture.

In the story "The National Theatre's Burning Down" a little Japanese press photographer keeps repeating 'Walesa, Wawel, Fibak, Walesa, Wawel, Fibak', attempting to summarize in this incantation all his knowledge about the country. The point, however, is that the inhabitants of the country behave no differently; they too attempt to encapsulate an element of self-knowledge in some slogan, sentence, or magic spell. Their situation is more difficult, though. The exotic visitor has his guide books; he knows where to find basic landmarks, is acquainted with the simplest hierarchies. They meanwhile wander blindly among trends, values and hierarchies that have been put to rout and whose ghosts now recall unreal stage-sets. So they talk feverishly, fretfully about cockroaches, committees and Kuroń, about defeat, victory, television, illness and the system. No one knows what is important, and what can be given a miss. No one knows where common sense begins, or where to find the magic formula. 'For years I could always find the key,' says one of the writers, 'it existed, it was ready-made. Now one has to write straight.'

All this is obviously controversial. Did the key exist, or didn't it? Should one or shouldn't one write straight, and for that matter does Anderman write straight? One thing, however, is beyond doubt: *The Edge of the World* is the perceptive and scathing record of a consciousness tragically lost in its quest for the Key, the Way, for Harmony; and the book heightens incertitude instead of allaying it. For who knows whether the stammering, spasmodic lamentation will really end in an epoch of universal silence (such as there has never been) or in an epoch of *glasnost* (which has been imminent more than once already).

Jerzy Pilch
Cracow, June 1988

(This essay appeared in *Tygodnik Powszechny*, a Catholic weekly published in Cracow. It was written as a review of *The Edge of the World* and has been edited slightly for a readership outside Poland.)

THE EDGE OF THE WORLD

Empty...Sort of

The taxi driver went up to the duty-room on cottonwool legs and stood quietly before the blurred pane with the round aperture. He twirled his cap in his hands and looked coaxingly at the duty-officer, who sat with his head collapsed on his chest. He looked like a man overcome by insurmountable drowsiness. But he was simply stooped over a small mirror set on his knee. A scrap of newspaper with a rosette of coagulated blood stuck to his upper lip; he was delicately trying to prize it away with the nail of his little finger.

— Excuse me, Sir, if you please.. — said the taxi driver, as he bowed low and froze in timeless obeisance.

The duty-officer shuddered and violently raised his head. The congealed drop of blood remained on his nail, a soft clank resounded under the table, and simultaneously atoms of light flashed in the semi-darkness.

— Seven years' bad luck — the taxi driver sheepishly volunteered, but was instantly scared by his own voice. The duty-officer looked at him, but manifested no irritation, as the scarlet streak that now joined the gash to the corner of his mouth caused him to smile rapaciously with half of his face.

— Well? — the duty-officer spoke. — Wha'?

1

— How to.. — the taxi driver at one jerk whipped off his cap — How to...I mean...is there any other exit?

— Wha'?

— I've got a passenger here, tall, cap, overcoat, I mean...said he'd be gone two minutes, but my meter's already clocked up a thousand seven hundred...and it's chilly...so maybe there's another exit here, or how...

— No one of that description came in 'ere today — the duty-officer said, grinding the glass with his boot.

— What d'ya mean no one of that description, when I saw him go in with my own eyes — for a moment the taxi driver lost his head, then instantly simmered down — I saw him go in. Cap and overcoat. Eight a.m. What time's it now? A thousand seven hundred on the meter. Chilly...isn't there another exit here, or...

— No one of that description came in 'ere today. Wait 'ere quietly or else go home. What I says I says. Yes or no. Got it?

The bewildered taxi driver reeled towards the door; what d'ya mean, no one came in when I saw him go in, had an overcoat, said stay put and wait, what d'ya mean when I tell you I saw him go in...it's like a movie, dammit, like a movie...a cap...

Two people passed him who without looking round proceeded along the familiar route to the blurred pane with the aperture. The taxi driver eyed them suspiciously and retreated to the door; it'll soon make a thousand seven hundred and forty — seven hundred and forty. Cold, eh?

The two men then tackled the stairs, the repellent metal netting climbed upwards above the banisters. The duty-officer sat behind the glass, staring down at the floor, at the carmine mouth of the actress whose photo

2

had come unstuck from the broken mirror. One might have thought he was blowing on his cold fingers. But he was only holding the receiver in his huge palm and reporting in dulcet tones — It's the, it's them two literary blokes summoned for...

And now they were instinctively but unnecessarily raising their heads to read the nameplates fastened above the doors, as they made their unerring way to the correct one.

They stopped outside, and when one of them raised his hand to knock, the door slid away from his fingers. For a moment they stood eye to eye, saying nothing, then they heard the instruction: I'm too busy right now, kindly wait on that bench for a while, we can have a chat later; they turned away towards the bench, retreating under an escort of eyes. Then they sat down and simultaneously leaned back on the bench as though a gust of wind from the closed doors had pushed them there.

They were silent, and the hard keyboard of the typewriter could be heard rattling away from the other side of the door.

Then for a long time the glow-lamp hissed beneath the ceiling, regularly died down, then returned after a moment. One of them took a newspaper from his pocket and glanced at the door, the other twirled a cigarette in his fingers spilling bits of tobacco, then placed it in his mouth without lighting up. They sat in silence, hemmed in by words that had already erupted earlier that day, on their way to this place.

They had been standing in a tramcar that dragged itself across the bridge so slowly the water beneath did not stir; it was in the paper, one of them said, about reducing the speed limit, people are inconvenienced by the noise, which in our language means the bridge is in danger of collapse; then the tram stopped and the door-wings flapped; smoke was belching from under the first wagon and when they go out, they saw a little woman in a tram conductor's cap rampaging down the car and yelling to the passengers, run for your lives, it'll be a right balls-up un' I don't know who's gunna pay, and as though to emphasize her words she banged the fire extinguisher on the asphalt; the extinguisher emitted a prolonged whistle, then after the last thump the bottom fell out, spilling a handful of rust from inside; people peered curiously under the car and for the first time that day their faces were creased with laughter; it's a sight for sore eyes, they whispered among themselves, smoking like the devil. They made for the river bank walking slowly, watching the exuberant water below; they passed the bays and the bridge ebbed away — I've never been so hamstrung by censorship as now, never; for the last couple of years it's been different, especially now; the old censor could be fooled in thousands of ways; the game could be fun, could be humiliating, but I don't know how to tackle this one; he's inside me, and he keeps getting stronger; he was pretty strong way back in '80 and '81, but in those days you simply waited, you could still suppress all your inner doubts; my censor made himself known in earnest when I was in jail; all those previously diffuse and elusive elements were concentrated in one place, several hundred people; it was a colony of apes; at first I resisted that image and rejected my own evaluation, but then the image took hold; besides, I wasn't alone. They hauled in a sober-minded bloke from the Poly and after a couple of days,

he realized how nauseated I was by all that jingoism,
all that ritual and religious singing every day through
the bars, stirring up the entire prison to a hunger strike
every other minute on the least pretext, and I saw great
tub-thumpers who noshed at night on the quiet and broke
those fasts of theirs after two days; that ranting on for
months on end about high-level politics, and "the spring
will be ours" even though the spring went on
relentlessly; the division between those who held that
the greatest service to the country was to take the mickey
out of the screw and those who went to give the screws
the season's greetings: that'll give 'em something to
think about, they'd say, and so another month was
twaddled away; plus those symbols, symbols of
something that no longer existed, because people didn't
have it inside them in the first place; so that sober bloke
from the Poly started telling how a legend was growing up about our prison in the outside world, people
were saying that the extreme of the extreme had been
rounded up here; as a rank-and-file activist he was glad
they'd taken him, he stood to learn a lot here in this
academy of the opposition; that's what he called it, now
he's just wondering how the whole business could ever
have lasted sixteen months; he couldn't get over his
amazement as he looked on and observed how a respec-
table union activist was happy if he caught sight of a
secret policeman in the yard, because he could shout
at him from a safe distance, you bastard, you broken
prick on duck's legs; he watched and was amazed and
wondered what could be gained by all that; he looked
at those people who gobbled the chocolate from foreign
parcels and then listened to children's stories about
ration cards for two hundred grams of lemon drops, and

that was an excuse for preaching about the ruthlessness of the authorities; he beheld a once-important guru whose mental laziness prevented his reassessing his view of his own importance; once he had conducted discussions about how the system encourages and fosters alcoholism, how the system depends on it, and here he had now discovered a way of distilling moonshine, and distilled it on the sly; he saw those who'd wanted to hang grafters now giving bribes to the man in charge of the baths who was serving a sentence for corruption, and for a douceur you can whistle a shirt with the prison stamp; it can be smuggled through at visiting hours; the women outside like to sport a grey shirt with the prison sign as a gesture of mourning; he saw them grumbling to the Swiss doctors from the Red Cross who've already seen a prison or two in Asia and South America; he heard them complaining that the water in the baths was too hot or too cold, he saw men who only recently had ordered others to paint graffiti about television lies, now sucking up to the screw so he'd let them watch the news out of turn; he saw politicals who treated the convicts with contempt; there were a couple of professional crooks in prison with us who went on hunger strike in sympathy, and it was entered in their personal files which would follow them through all the prisons of the land all their lives long, he saw people who were happy to be in prison and did not notice their halo was of scurf; so that sober-minded fellow told me that, though he considers himself to be a cultured type, he would formulate his view as follows — namely, he wouldn't give a shit for such an academy of opposition. Obviously not everything there was so bad, there were lots of different people, but somehow it all got blurred and that

6

ghastly image prevailed; I ended up not writing a single word about those days, because either my censor would have made a liar of me unto death, since you simply couldn't write about such things; the idea was to build morale and boost myths regardless, and for a book like that — had I ever got round to writing — I'd have received the Ministry of Culture prize at least, or worse. Besides, what publisher would have printed it? I'd have been treated like a provocateur or police spy...

They paced their walk slowly from bay to bay, as the bridge receded, and they were soon to stand on firm, hard ground. — I find reading difficult, I pick up a book with a sense of nausea; it looks as though the garbage dump will become literature, and nothing else will remain, all those hundreds of pages, thousands of poems, memoirs, diaries, impressions, notes, all very soulful and high-minded, those sufferings endured with slimy satisfaction; how many more years is this to be our nourishment? Those December nights, wars declared on the entire nation, nothing less would do, tanks, handcuffs, armoured cars, troops going out on the street, all those stage props, even private dreams under martial law, and children's thoughts for posterity; that specific language one is duty-bound to use if one wants to belong; it's our own newspeak; those internment camps, reds, bolshies, underground broadsheets, police ambushes, raids; even those held in unbarred rooms in vacation centres refer to them as cells and camps; loss of freedom is not enough, what matters is the rig-out; when I read all that stuff I feel like puking, there's not so much as a thought on the horizon; like throwing petrol bombs at water-cannons, and there's no breaking free, for there's no tolerance here; pathos excludes tolerance and we're getting close to using hopeless propaganda, just one step from the method and gimmicks of the other side, just one step from their mentality and stereotypes, their stultification and absolutism; one mag had the guts to discuss these problems; people started shouting that it was a secret police job and I don't know if the publication's still coming out; it all makes me puke, I've had my own small part in it, but I'll probably pack it, though it's difficult to go it alone, to hell with all this foambeating; up-fingers is the only universally adopted program to be invariably shown — that's our form of salute...

They stopped for a moment and rested against the rail; I'd gladly toss a coin into the water, one of them said, it might help me reassess a couple of problems, for either I calmly go on considering myself the aristocrat of literature or else I finally admit that the literary backwater, that provincial homespun stuff, is me; that's really what our literature is; our whingeing behind prison bars and our obtusely menacing squeaks about the spring being ours sound like poetry to us; we have nurtured censors within us who have outstripped us and our thoughts and write on our behalf about this country; we're happy from time to time to get a parcel from abroad with a kilo of sugar, a kilo of flour and some toothpaste; we'd gladly frame the parcel as documentary proof that Europe remembers and admires Polish literature; admirable people, noble nation gone to the dogs, we describe it in our own blood, but we write on blank cards dealt out by our censor; it was this censor who prevented my writing that I didn't want any hero's testimony; everyone in my prison was handed a testimony; a souvenir for life, they said with emotion, a pass to history, they said hysterically, good typographic design and half-bound what's more...

They reached the tramstop on the bridge that joined the two banks and suddenly stopped talking, as though they felt hard ground underfoot. One of them pointed at the colossal building and the huge red flag full-sail above it, and white-capped young men milling all around. And we'll carry on about how they sit there plotting which scenario to apply, but in the event we shall die standing, not on our knees. The wheels screeched. Their tram rolled up to the stop in a veil of smoke. Clearly the woman with the conductor's cap falling over her eyes had lost heart and was now staring indifferently ahead with blank expression. They boarded and the tramcar immediately dissolved in a black fog.

Afterwards they sat in silence. One of them put his newspaper away, and the other drew out his next cigarette and crushed it between his fingers. It was the twentieth cigarette he had not lit during the long hours waiting on the bench that day.

The glow-lamp hissed beneath the ceiling, the light flared, then expired. A man in overalls appeared in the aisle. He walked swiftly towards them, and drew up suddenly in passing.

— Just a moment — he said without giving them a look.

They sprang up in surprise; two more steps, two more steps, one more, said the man, and when they had moved a little to the side he pushed the bench away. Behind it there was a small metal door in the wall, which he opened. He took a screw driver from his pocket and started fiddling among the cables, tapping the microphone head. Then he glanced at them and at the cables again and shrugged his shoulders; what the fuck do they want, he muttered, everything's OK. He slammed the metal door, pushed the bench back in place and made off. He turned round for one moment longer and flung over his shoulder, Quiet, aren't we?

Then the door opened and there stood the man who'd ordered them to wait. As it happens, he said I'm quite snowed under, so we might as well call it a day. Should the occasion arise, then of course…He tapped his finger against the door-frame and closed the door behind him.

Exhausted and relieved, they went downstairs slowly; I began to feel the urge, one of them said, it's a neat situation to describe, but I thought you might want to. They descended to the landing and turned into the broad staircase; I did have the urge, only I thought less in terms of situation than of storyline, besides I thought I'd let you have it as you might feel inclined, the second one said, and that we'd sort it out between us when we left…

And they both started laughing and laughing, and they came to the room where the duty-officer sat behind the blurred aperture, and still they were laughing; the pale taxi driver stood muttering to himself by the wall; he must have come in, I saw him with my own eyes, I've clocked up four thousand two hundred, four and two hundred; you definitely didn't see him, he shouted to the duty-officer in despair. But the latter looked at the men laughing, pulled the visor over his eyes and lifted his head, because he could now see them only knee-high.

— What're ya laughin' at, huh? Who 're ya laughin' at?

— Ourselves — one of them replied.

Quietly they closed the heavy door behind them.

— Well — the duty-officer shook his fist after

them. — Well. Loonies, eh? — he turned to the taxi driver.

— No, no, it's from Gogol — the taxi driver instinctively mumbled.

The National Theatre's Burning Down

A banner of flame streams from the National Theatre and is smothered in smoke. Sanguine pigeons sway above the marsh of rooftops like small black sails and search frantically for their old roosts.

At the roof's edge several firemen clutch a limp hose, waiting for water. They lift their legs above the abyss like cancan girls as the sheetiron burns their soles. The firemen glance indifferently at the eyes frozen in admiration below, eyes that gaze in horror: a fireman has misstepped and beats his arms as if to warm himself. But it's clear that he's flapping his arms to regain his balance, and his life. The crowd groans relief as, in the last instant, the fireman grabs the flabby hose, straightens up, spits into the fire, and glances down at the street.

The low sky is propped on billowing pillars of smoke.

In the theatre square motionless red cars and yellow watering-vans with snowplows secured to their fronts deliver water from the town. Large-helmeted firemen storm among the cars and the swirl of hoses; a dentil of police separates them from the crowd. The policemen are young and eager, their visors screening the curiosity and desperation in their eyes; they're not allowed to face the raging fire, nor to take a single step forward. So they stand in a trance, questioning the people's faces, trying to discover what is going on behind their own backs. They do not see the small group of actors in fantastical costumes driven out of rehearsal by the flames and who now give feverish interviews to the camera: — I was just standing there, and suddenly the stage rode up in the air, and there was a great swoosh, and I just fled. And now I'm not budging an inch from here.

— And I even lost my shoes, I've got no shoes, oh god, I've lost my shoes — another one keened, forever pointing at his feet. — See what I mean, I don't even have shoes. What a fizzle.

— As for myself, in all honesty, I thought the ventilation'd turned on again, so I shouted to them to turn it off, what a hope, some ventilation that is, heaven help us.

— Our home sweet home's on fire — the actors now cry, and gather like a small flock of exotic birds. That last shout pierces the ranks of the vigilant militiamen and reaches the crowd; people nod their heads in approval and look at each other knowingly. — That's it, that's it, fire is a vicious element, say what you like.

— A flaming red fire, begging your pardon.

— Hey, listen — a man in the crowd chips in — you know, at ten a.m. Radio Free Europe said it was burning, so I dashed along, and the fire started at half past twelve. So how could they have known at ten? Because extremists told them their plans beforehand, but couldn't keep on schedule. It's all clear. The underground did it. And how! How could they know . . .

People turn their gaze from the fire, lower their heads, adjust to the sudden dimness and look for the man who'd been speaking, but he surfaces elsewhere, emerges from the crowd, explains heatedly, gesticulating, pointing behind him. — That lot heard Free Europe giving news of the fire at ten

14

a.m. They can confirm it. And the fire broke out at half-past twelve, now didn't it? Everybody heard.

— Well, sort of — uncertain voices respond.

— So what the hell's going on here? — someone reflects out loud.

— Extremists set it alight. The underground. Simple, ain't it?

— Just which undergound are you talking about? It's obvious who did it. Mijal's gang. Anyone can tell you that.

— But Mijal's in the jug. It was in the papers.

— Right you are. When were you born? It's like talking to a small child. So what if he is? He's got a network all over Poland. Every national theatre will go up in flames now. First it was the castle, now the theatres, next the... He who steals an egg will steal an ox, you mark my words.

— And Kuron, he said not to burn cummittees. To build cummittees — someone says, then becomes petrified and breaks into nervous uncontrollable laughter.

— It's the undergound what done it.

— What bullshit he talks. It's provoca...

— There's different ways of looking at it — people start putting two and two together. — When the fire broke out Bujak was seen in disguise. Sure was.

— Who saw him?

— Everyone...

— You did too?

— I didn't actually, I came late. Everyone else did though. He was in uniform to dodge the police. He's grown a beard. Just slipped past.

Suddenly a tapering flame cuts through the film of smoke. A group of women suddenly begin to wail like orphans:
— *God that hast Po-o-o-land throughout all the ce-e-enturies*
— the choir swells, the song drifts like smoke only to fall

15

an instant later, the words become unhinged and disjointed, and quarrelsome voices can be heard again — it's not allowed, the primate forbade us to sing *Give us back our free land*, so what if he did, seeing it's not free anyway, let's sing as it comes, we're not to sing, sing bless oh lord, the primate said not to sing that version, but the correct one — smoke stifles the fretful voices, people watch as the last victims descend the tapering ladder. Trapped by the fire, they'd been patiently waiting at the windows to be rescued; at the foot of the ladder the commander admonishes a smoke-black fireman guarding the only escape route — For chrissake, don't let 'em in, let 'em out, don't let 'em in — The fireman stands to attention, senses the numerous eyes focused on him and blinks uncertainly at the crowd — Firemen aren't up to much nowadays, they used to be better-looking, more like men, they're not up to much nowadays, flashy uniforms all right, they were better-looking before...

— They used to get plenty of sauerkraut and pease pudding in the old days. More lime, better teeth. Now there's less lime. And no sauerkraut to be had for love or money.

Drunk at this early hour, a man hoists a baby in a polyester jump suit aloft to show him the fire — Let the kid learn from the cradle — he explains to his neighbours; the frisky infant in his slippery outfit keeps sliding out of the man's uncertain grip — For all the world like a little eel, a slippery little eel — the man says admiringly. Exhilarated by the crowd, two young girls at his side quite unashamedly read a crumpled clandestine newsheet; the miniature rheostats rise and fall with their breasts.* — Here, says one with flushing cheeks, here, Solidariusz has won, see? Solidariusz has won! It all

* Worn to signify resistance to the regime after Solidarity badges were banned. (Translator's note)

16

began in '83, when Mr Jagiello decided to give his son the names Przemyslaw Solidariusz. The People's Council refused to register him, invoking the opinion of the Linguistic Culture Committee. Then there was a scission. Chairman Professor Szymczak objected to the name Solidariusz, while the vice-chairman and two members of the presidium backed the child's father. The case went to the Chief Administrative Court. Mr Jagiello won, but the People's Council still refused to register the name. The father appealed and despite fierce resistance on the part of the prosecutor, the court again recognized the father's claim. The People's Council finally gave way and the boy was officially named Solidariusz.

— The ranks of our defence grow day by day — people mutter admiringly. — There's nothing they're afraid of. Now they'll seize the stick. The proverbial stick. We've already done our share of the fighting.

— Old folks won't be laying down arms that easily. Oh no they won't. We'll show 'em the stuff we're made of. Tit for tat, a stick for a stick. Why, it can't be more than an hour ago, women began making a cross of flowers, under the eyes of the police, but they only had enough flowers for one arm. With the police watching 'em. If we had more flowers, we'd give'em what for...

— Some fire that.

— First they start a fire, now they'll pretend there's no water to extinguish it. They've brought the plows out. The plows, I ask you.

— There's more than one way of looking at it. At any rate the director's office knew nothing, because the managing director was cut in half by the safety curtain, in the presence of witnesses; there's an iron curtain like I'm saying in case of fire, or rather there was, because it's melted now; the director dashed forward to lower it and seal off the flames, but the ropes burned through and whang bang it chopped him in two on the spot, in two equal halves it did; one half was consigned to flames, the other to water, courtesy of the fire brigade. It's tragic, I must say.

— It's an act of God. 'Cause a couple of years ago that director said on the radio that Witkacy committed suicide on hearing that the Germans had invaded Poland.* That's divine judgement for you. He had another two years to go, not a bad run for his money if you ask me. He just made the centenary and then croaked.

— The angel wings in the costume wardrobe are burned to a frazzle.

— Hussars' wings, not angel wings.

— There's no Hussar wings, what rubbish you do talk. Angel wings, I tell you. Quite apart from the fact that lots of people have been burned. Couldn't escape in time, burned to a frazzle. And people of standing what's more.

— See the women with a portrait of St Florian, the fire doesn't seem so bad over there. The way things are, there's nothing the fire brigade can do. There's nothing doing. I'm going back home, just waiting for the opera to catch fire.

— There's no help for it now. That's what happens when brother raises arms against brother.

A gust of wind made a gap in the smoke and people again craned their stiffened necks to watch the fireman with taut hoses and silvery chords of water slipping from their grasp. The crowd had laughing eyes and were reluctant to turn from the scene, when suddenly excitement rustled nearby. A little Japanese gent slipped out of the crowd clutching a shiny

* The modernist painter and playwrite Witkacy committed suicide three weeks later in fact, when the Russians invaded Poland.

movie camera; he raised the lens high and stepped back, for the weight was too much and he had trouble keeping his balance. — Siogun, siogun — cries rose from the crowd — you there, siogun, sepulu sake san... And the Japanese gent turned his little face, which was wrinkled like a paradise apple, and bowed to the people. — It's Japanese TV. It'll show the whole truth — the gent nodded rhythmically, Walesa, Walesa, he said to the people standing by him, Walesa, Wawel, Fibak, and they raised their hands with fingers outspread, nodding their heads in agreement, toranaga, toranaga, kilder, ja, ja, guten...

The Japanese stepped back in fear, as someone grabbed his sleeve and began hectoring him. — We won't surrender, you tell your people, whatever they do, we give them what for, tit for tat it is, and they're not going to win by burning our sanctuaries — and the little fellow retreated into the crowd shielding himself with the long lens of his camera. The man moved doggedly in his tracks, was now poised just above his eardrum, whispering in deep intimacy — They say Pekala's escaped from prison and is getting his own back...

A woman with diluted features was sitting on a scrap of tar-paper on the curb, so stout she might've been dipped in a bladder of opaque fluid; she had a child's plastic toy piano by her; her swollen fingers fumbled over the keys and she sang, and people tossed coins into an empty, coloured cola can propped against the split upper of her gumboot — *Then the screw breaks in the cell, The prisoner he starts to beat, The prisoner falls on his face, And his heart then stops to beat, Then we're all dragged out by night*... — Coins drop into the can and tap out the rhythm, someone tugs at the drunkard plunged in purple dreams on a park bench — Mister, I say get up mister, you've slept through the best part of it; that's good; what's good is it'll stir the conscience of Europe, words can be heard — and for a moment the little drunkard raises his eyelids to reveal white eyeballs, and whispers — Paint me at calvary...

— Things can't be left the way they are and now a group of former internees has prepared a letter of protest to the authorities. They've collected signatures, but only among themselves. — The firemen deploy the ladders and unroll the thin hoses — Try the other side, try the other side — someone advises them from the crowd — tackle it from the side and smother the heart of the fire — smoke enfolds the firemen and absorbs the voice of the crazed man who's shaking his fists at them and spitting pink foam with his words — flunkeys, flunkeys,...henchmen...

The crowd sways restlessly and turns its back on the conflagration to face a cavalcade of black Tchaikas and Volgas swooping along the roadway. Round faces with puffed and slanted eyes stare morosely ahead, white behind the murky panes; an instant later the raven-black cars vanish beyond the bend, hounded by shouts, jeers and curses.

— We must, I mean we really must let Wajda know so he can bring his gear; he can use it afterwards in a film, the National Theatre, today's the March anniversary and you're not telling me it's an accident — a feverish voice is heard and a hand wipes a tear from a cheek. The people around blink, startled by the white light of someone's camera-flash, which poses the flames and smoke against the backdrop of the sky.

A woman holding a squashed hotdog sits on the bench by the drunkard plunged in a malignant fever; grey mushroom sauce trickles onto her knees, but she pays no attention and bites the soggy breadroll and says to the sleeping drunk — I've come from Kielce, spent half the day tramping round town, thinking I'd chance upon the General but I was out of luck, I wanted to so bad, banked on it I did, I've worn my feet out, I deserve a treat, 'cause I've come from Kielce, all the way from Kielce — and he raises an eyelid and gives a sober glance and replies — yeah, sure, work is for fools, piss-artist rules; mind you, the wops show sex a treat — and his head slowly slips back between the tails of his coat.

From the roof of a neighbouring house a white flock takes flight, swoops above the square, till sucked in by a gust of hot air it spins skywards and vanishes in the thick smoke. The KPN's dropped leaflets — people whisper the news — it's the KPN — the militiamen twitch uneasily, but they're not allowed to shift places, so they frisk the crowd with their eyes, and an old gypsy woman, garishly dressed, threads her way past the cordon and fawns to the idle officials — Hey you, ginger, give us a coin for ripeness, you there ginger, give us a coin for the belly . . .

— The Coordination Bureau's already issued a communiqué, somebody here heard from the monitoring — says a man chafing his hands.

The theatre is now thoroughly hobbled with hoses, the firemen climb the ladders like acrobats without holding on, and when they reach the windows they furiously thwack their hatchets at the panes; the dark glass showers the mouldings.

— I'm telling you, the church guard ought'a be called in to restore order. I've got a church guard helmet at home, I could fetch it in just half a sec, couldn't I?

And the firemen, spurred on by the vast eye of the crowd, vanish one after the other in the plush of smoke.

Mauve rays dart from the lights on the car roofs and flit over the motionless faces; eyes brighten then go dim; chilled to the bone, people mechanically stomp their feet — Fancy making someone stand out in this cold. That lot at least are in the warm. It's like an ice-box down here. An ice-box, I tell you.

— The worst thing about it is that truth won't out, as the saying goes. It'll all be hidden from the public eye, as the saying goes.

— Begging your pardon, I don't know what they see in this marxism of theirs. Not in this leninism either, begging your pardon.

The National Theatre's ablaze, the crowd remains rooted in the square below and only one man begins to fight his way out of the enclosure; people reluctantly let him pass — Where on earth, it's not over yet, where...

— I'm dashing home, it's soon time for the first news on the box. Gotta go. Whatever else, they're bound to show the fire.

Poland Still?

Bells ring above the bulk of the church; swifts swish, black glints against the pargetted wall. Down below, the square expands as a massive crowd pours from the church, then overflows in all directions and stops dead, helpless, sapped of all energy. Darkness rises in the warm breaths, swallows the walls and climbs slowly toward the towers, till the muffled bell dies away.

The crowd is alone.

The crowd is alone and doesn't know what to do with itself, which way to turn, whom to bawl at or what demands to make. It is tired, crumpled and undecided. It's not the crowd it was, and people eye one another with distrust.

A handful of people like specks of dust break away from the crowd; furtively they unpin the coloured badges on their coats, crowned eagles that could gouge out alien eyes. Compliantly they clench their fingers and nimbly pick their way between the serried ranks of silent militiamen; they dart off to the nearby bus-stops; they want to lie low at home and forget.

The crowd remains rooted.

People scrutinize one another; not to fall apart, not to disperse, to stay put, stay put; there is after all a chance, a settlement could be reached...

— Settle what...

23

— Well, try and settle all the issues...
— What issues do you mean...
— Well, to discuss...
— Discuss what...
— Well, formulate...
— Formulate what...
— Well, decide everything...
— Decide what...
— Well, coordinate everything...
— But with whom...
— Well, with them...
— With them...
— Not with them... With the others...
— It's high time to coordinate...
— And definitely postulate...
— Absolutely, absolutely...

A husky amplified voice floats out from an undefined point in the dark towards the crowd — Disperse peacefully, go home, don't form groups, disperse, otherwise we shall have to resort to... — There's a riot on the way, a man whispers, a riot...

— Time to start?
— Start what?
— Poland Still?*
— Poland Still?
— Well...
— Not yet, not yet...

At a safe distance from here a hunched silhouette cowers behind a windowpane — Meduz calling, Meduz calling; it'll probably move, a crowd's formed and now it's waiting, it'll

* The Polish national anthem begins, "Poland still has not perished/As long as we are alive."

24

probably move; the blues've lined the square, they're in control; no curses or abuse for the time being, no shouting; right now it's singing *Give us back, o lord* or something like that, but in patches, in patches; the situation calls for water cannon; when it moves give'em water cannon for a scare; some of 'em are laughing and gaping, hey, some are already giving the salute and there's our little eye recording it all, and now I can hear *We'll not desert the land* and *You sovietized our kids*; I can see old women and youngsters making the V-sign to one another and laughing; I can see one fellow with a lens recording it all, but it's not one of ours, it's coloured, gaudy as a parrot, he'll be recorded by our lens and he'll have to be checked outside the precincts; the blues are standing quietly by waiting for the kick-off, and then there'll be water for a scare...

Voices rage more and more distinctly above the crowd, beads of mist settle on bare heads, a helicopter hovers in the darkness and coarsely grinds the dense air. — Grandpa, a ten-year-old boy asks, say Grandpa, what was it like in Walesa's time? In Walesa's time, to be perfectly honest — the old man strains his eyes — to tell you the truth it wasn't that simple. There's more than one way. It varied like. One way and the other. That's what. Something like.

And standing aside, the faceless reporter formulates his version for tomorrow morning's news bulletin and asks himself who drove this handful of disoriented youngsters, kids really, to demonstrate; who are the bosses cowering behind the youngsters' backs; who wanted to plant this arsenal of dirty tricks on Polish soil; who lined Geremek's and Michnik's pockets with fat wads of Bonn marks, London pounds, Washington dollars and other foreign currencies; we all know only too well the answers to these and other problems that spring inevitably to the minds of the broad masses of indignant citizens, who in their overwhelming majority daily voice their support. To the disrupters of dialogue and partisans of Star Wars, the spokesmen of national reconciliation resolutely say no. The reporter peers cautiously about him and sees loathsome faces that disgust him. Not long ago he had to repent in sackcloth and ashes before these people, making tearful promises, and he'll never forget his humiliation, never get over that stifling hatred. He fears the crowd and the future.

The collective silence is ominous, and the foreign reporter is also afraid of the crowd; she looks at the crowd, no longer knowing if those faces staring white in the darkness are wild and Asiatic or gentle and wisely European; she is fascinated by the crowd, and excited by it; she is in its midst, and at the same time embraces the thousands; she sees two, then four, five and ten thousand; she would hug them to her breast; she ignores the hostile blue lane, for she is a Western reporter; she is untouchable and besides, the communists in Nicaragua did her no harm, she wasn't trampled during the carnival in Havana, so she must get to the bottom of this lot too; thoughts scurry through her brain without her being able to fix on any; a defeat that's not a defeat, a victory that's not a victory, a defeat that'll be a victory, a victory that'll be a victory; she sees an old woman being shunted along by an equally ancient and jaded old boy and hears the woman shouting some words in that strange withered-ivy language that rustles warmly on her parched lips, and the reporter gives the old woman a friendly smile, nods vivaciously and stabs the air with her forked fingers — Listen, the woman shouts out, listen; you think you're badly off, do you? What more do you want? Two televisions each? Three? Did you have those TVs before the war? No, you didn't. Bloody hell!

— Hold it! You right bitch — the man says. — You ain't

got a pennyworth of shame...

— Bitch. Bitch. That's all you can say. How many TVs can a man have, when all's said and done?

The edge of the crowd is lined by church guardians in tall caps that look like Uhlan shakos from a distance; the guardians penetrate the crowd; some of them stand motionless and stare at the ZOMO men without a word; and without a word the ZOMO men return the stare.

— Maybe now's the time for Poland Still?

— What?

— Poland Still?

— Poland Still, Poland Still! Not yet...

Voices are borne from end to end of the crowd, which stays put, waiting, not budging an inch; helmets gleam dangerously close, for the time being they hold, stock still as the paving stones; the waiting goes on until from somewhere among the treetops or the church roof muffled words break loose and ripple amid the crowd — What's he saying, what's he saying, that voice; it's the underground speaking on tape, it's a tape; but what's he saying, what's that voice —

we shall   we celebrate   not lay down   festival
      we remember   solemnly   as always
the August   we must   festival   the December
    we'll give   festival   inflexibly   our reply
      achievements   festival   we pledge
   ceremony   our communal   we'll clench
      festival   we persist   we reject
we recall
      festival   sign our pacts   and postulate
    standing   festival   festive   festival
      celebrat   celebrat   celeb

— Well, are we getting on with it, or aren't we; what're we supposed to — people ask the voice, but the voice can't

hear; words float through the crowd, the echo lifts them back
into the air, into the dark and the mist; the words bounce
off the poet; the poet isn't listening, because he's doing his
level best to compose a poem that will bear witness, the poet
remembers; today the bells are ringing, sounding the alarm,
the crowd outside the church, hope kindled in its hearts, while
the red dragon in the sky, flaps its real tail in vain, in vain
it sends its cohorts in; and the poet pauses awhile as the rhyme
for cohorts eludes him, what rhymes with cohorts; cohorts
reports; janissaries, mercenaries; but Poland still has to be
fitted in, phalanx black hundreds tatars mortars, there's still
nothing to rhyme with Poland . . . so the poet leaves the rhyme
for later, and for the time being constructs a couplet, repeating
the words with emphasis for fear they give him the slip
— Rejoice not, vicious dragon red; the day we fight you'll
soon be dead . . .

— Well folks, what are we doing — someone asks in an
unnaturally loud voice — seeing as we're doing nothing, we'd
better be snappy. The guardians in the chef's-hat helmets stalk
the crowd with their eyes; people retreat respectfully just in
case; they exchange swift glances and slight motions of the
head; the man over there is silent beyond recall and someone
else, wanting to smooth over the situation, explains coaxingly:
— I might even get the truncheon. Better still. Let England
know. Then we'll see. England must say stop. Either there's
some justice in the world, or there isn't.

A woman squeezes her way deftly through the crowd; she
is wearing trousers and a blue sweater and a too-small cap
with a pompom on a thread that bobs about like a yoyo; she
peers into the bystanders' eyes and whispers — Hungar fruit
drops, Hungar bubblegum, what, fruit drops, fruit drops . . .

— Wouldn't mind some of the bubble stuff, but it depends
how much — someone mutters mechanically, but he makes

28

no move and the woman's voice drifts into the distance and a child tugs hopefully at its mother's sleeve, and she says without looking in a tone of torment, get off my sleeve, get off my sleeve, or I'll knock you off.

— So what's up?

— How d'you mean what's up?

— When's the speech?

— It's already been.

— How come? When?

— Why ask? Ought've listened...

— When was the speech?

— Wakey wakey — the man unexpectedly replies, and looking round in triumph, he breaks out into prolonged uncontrollable laughter that blocks his windpipe.

— Must be time for Poland Still?

— What?

— How about Poland Still?

— Poland Still...not yet...

The foreign television team probes the crowd with its lens. A correspondent swathed in a coloured scarf adopts a professional air and hustles the cameraman for good measure. Make sure you show the church helping Solidarity. It's a must.

— I know my job.

— It must be made clear. When you did the prison, you were meant to show the political prisoners. And all you could see was walls, bare walls. Nothing to show it was political. Just bars and rooftops.

— I did it myself — says the cameraman, offended.

— There's nothing to get uptight about — the correspondent says. — If you did it, then that's OK. Can you see how the church is being supportive?

— Clear as day.

— Well then, we'll be off.

— Couldn't we perhaps wait for the bloodshed?

— Bloodshed, ah, bloodshed. The trouble with bloodshed...

The crowd waits patiently; shouts and scraps of songs sparkle in the darkness; words reverberate against the plastic shields of the impenetrable militia.

Again the loudspeaker is heard from the roof of a car slowly driving round the posts and cordons — I appeal to you to disperse.

— By the church they can't touch us.

— They won't enter the precincts. We're immune.

— Not here they won't. Out there it's different.

— Out there they would.

The crowd is rooted but will probably soon move under the batons, it has no other way out.

Here and there banners open like flowers.

The crowd stirs, no one asks where, it won't get far anyway.

The crowd knows it will be routed and will achieve nothing. But it sallies forth because it has no other way of honouring today's anniversary. So the crowd celebrates the way it knows best.

A stone's throw from here asylum ends at the black asphalt and the rasping loudspeaker on the car roof. There's a cordon ahead waiting to receive the crowd.

Faces are now turned in the opposite direction, rage and despair and fear swell in the helpless people, mouths are rent by more and more cries.

— Flunkeys!

— Gestapo!

— Bandits!

— Scroungers!

— Fascists!

— Anti-Poles!

— Red plague!

— Butchers!

— Renegades!

The disciplined ranks give a faint shudder, but do not stir from their posts. The transparent visors drop with a clatter and a glass wall of shields rears up.

The crowd waves, sways, swells.

And suddenly the first drops fall, followed by an abundant rain of coins; the crowd chucks fistfuls of small change at the motionless ranks; the coins glitter in the lamplight like a shoal of fish on the move.

The ranks withdraw not a step; the rain slowly abates, the crowd soon discards its loose change; people breathe helplessly and watch...

Single huddled silhouettes break away from the crowd; their numbers increase as people watch speechless; they stoop dutifully before the cordon; they are within the batons' reach; they crouch low and eagerly scoop up the coins and stuff them into their pockets; elderly fingers fumble feverishly in the mud.

— Disperse singly to your homes! — cries the loudspeaker on the car roof.

Brightened by the falling coins, the darkness slowly fades.

— Friends, look friends, how could you...

— Why ask, why ask... You'll be old too one day. And you'll just have a pension to live on. Then you'll see. Just you wait...

— You have to make ends meet somehow...

Pockets stuffed, indifferent, the pensioners carry their booty into the crowd.

— Now?

31

— What now?
— Poland Still?
— Poland Still? Any minute now.
The crowd stirs.

VICTO...

That day was just like any other, it washed the clotted square as before; people dodged between the cars towards the bus-stops, wedged their way into shops and huddled round the ice-coated window of the commissary with its transistor radio and gleaming asiatic teaspoons; the window-dresser had thrown in a snakeskin and some cotton shirts with purple hearts and English wording I love New York, I love London, smile, kiss me; people fought silently for vantage points to gape at the objects, and a child whispered beseechingly to its father — Oh let's go now, let's go and have a look at the hard currency stores; the nearest ones are in Graniczna Street, in Stawki, Intrako, in Piwna Street and there's one in the Hotel Europe, just two stops away; and tomorrow we can still go to Jerusalem Avenue, the Forum and the Polonia...

A frozen vendor in a pointed cap made of newspaper stood motionless by his soda-water dispenser; the slogan *Proletarians of the World* ran across his forehead only to vanish behind his ear, and a raspberry icicle the size of a stalactite hung from the dispenser tap; the vendor thrummed it thoughtfully like a harp string... He appeared to be dozing with his head askew and muttering in his sleep; he was in fact squinting at the polished surface of the dispenser, in which his newspaper cap and the newsprint were reflected, and he slowly mouthed the words that were reflected backwards as in a mirror and which he read in reverse...six small elephants — donated — by Cuba — arrived — in a temperature — of minus — thirty — at Moscow — zoo. They sailed — to Leningrad — wrapped — in warm — woolly blankets. — They travelled from — Leningrad — to — Moscow — in — specially — heated — railway — coaches — and — from — Moscow — station — to — the — zoo — in heated — cars. — They arrived in fine form: He tugged nervously on the raspberry icicle and it fell with a clang onto the wording reflected on the table-top, crossing it through with a red line... — Mother-fucker, oh, mother-fucker, the vendor whispered white-mouthed, and the day drifted and wavered above the square and dragged in its wake days and months and years to come...

No one knew when it happened; in a split second white caps sprouted at the exit of the square, countless whistles tore the day and blocked the way to cars; nimble white wristbands waved them impatiently off, people slipped warily away; a bus slowly rolled into a sidestreet, and the bewildered passengers, whisked off in an unknown direction, flung mute curses from behind glass and helplessly shook their fists...

As though struck unawares by a gust of wind the square emptied quickly, silence fell upon silence, militiamen appeared so suddenly they might've stepped out from the plasterwork, they surrounded the square, sauntering about with feigned nonchalance, a bunch of people who had nowhere to hide stayed put on the bus-stop island, they continued standing there and really couldn't care and didn't even look up to see what had disrupted their day; nearby a lopsided taxi dug into the ground, it couldn't be hauled from the square as it had only three wheels to stand on; the fourth wheel lay alongside the chassis, the bewildered taxi driver stared at it and stooped and gently fingered it, then straightened up again and kicked it with rage, and a breathless woman ran across the empty square; with the last remnant of her strength she ran up to the taxi and tugged at the door; the three-wheeled vehicle keeled like a boat; the driver gazed at the crowd for a long while, then said — If that was a man, he'd be no more than a heap of rubble now . . . and as things are . . . — and he dropped on his knees by the wheel and froze in that posture.

A green bus entered from a side street, came to a halt and began to churn out soldiers with musical instruments; the leader shouted protracted orders, and his bargehauler's voice gave shape to the amorphous mass; an instant later there were no more people; a quadrangle stood to attention in the square and upon imbibing the last command it lurched forward and set off toward the middle of the empty square, where there were stone steps and a plinth bearing a gigantic figure with a metal cloak covered in greenish patina and clutching a metal book in its metallic right palm . . .

The quadrangle marched up to the figure without reducing its pace and had it not been for the sudden command that stopped it in its tracks, it might even have overturned that metallic giant . . .

A militiaman stood motionless surveying the people on the island, waited, and failed to see his uniformed colleague steal up behind him; he crept closer and closer, then pounced, landed him a mighty thump and like an eagle-owl hooted down his eardrum hoo-hoo; the militiaman leaped about, his first reflex was to grab his cap for fear of losing it, and grip his baton and pistol, only to freeze in his tracks; his colleague eyed him condescendingly, nodded his head and barked — What, 'fraid of the militia, mate? — and gave such a laugh that a passenger at the bus-stop shuddered as though wrenched out of a dream...

The military quadrangle froze; wind, frost and dust dulled the golden glints of the musical instruments, and at the bus-stop people stood not even wondering how long they would have to wait; they stood because they had taken up positions; the place was no worse than any other, no one was kicking them out. And so they stood.

Women held their heads confidentially close — And so I tell him he's not to speak to me like that, so he tells me not to tell him, so I tell him to belt up; you mean to say you said that to him, what did he say to that; well, so I told him how he should speak to me, I tell you it's always, well, so to speak...

The taxi driver jacked up the car and was helplessly fitting the wheel, which kept falling away — Know the one about children and the windshield wipers? — a voice piped up — children and windshield wipers...

— Windshield wipers?

— Right. Turn on the windshield wipers when the brakes fail.

— What? What the devil?

— You know, mister. The blood. To scrape the guts from the pane. And the blood.

— Don't you try telling me that bullshit.

— Haven't much sense of humour, have we? None whatsoever — the voice sounds offended, then falls silent.

People blinked as flashing blue lights wreathed the square, lights that danced along the house walls only to fade in mid-air in a perpendicular siberia of clouds; a cavalcade of gleaming Mercedes and Volgas and Tchaikas and Ladas slipped soundlessly into the square; chauffeurs in smart caps leaped out and obligingly opened doors; the square buzzed and blushed with bright-coloured wreaths; in the wink of an eye the newcomers lined up, each perfectly in place; the line stood at ease, fidgeted momentarily, then froze in position; the display was spoiled by the somewhat protruding figure of a black man shivering so violently from cold that he kept jerking about; but the rank promptly drew him in and order was resumed; the rank froze, stood to attention and music blared from the quadrangle; the taxi driver didn't so much as glance in its direction.

— There'll be special deliveries to the shops, I bet.

— What a hope. Not for the likes of that. Not a ghost of a . . .

— For the Revolution they will, with luck.

— Not for the Revolution they won't. More likely for Rebirth. If anything.

— Rebirth's more than six months to go. But it's a dead cert. They can't fail to, not for Rebirth they can't.

— And if they don't, so what? Fuckin' great mongrel.

The music swayed above the square, and the first threesome clutching a wreath stepped out of the row heading for the greenish metal figure as drums rolled like dried peas underfoot; a soldier led them like blind men though the three pairs of slanting eyes knew the way full well; finally they halted, two soldiers received the wreath, worried over it at the foot of the plinth, and the red-tongued sashes blew about in the wind; the wreath at last settled, the soldiers stood to attention, the threesome stood awhile apparently counting to ten, then together bowed its three heads before the plinth and walked back to take up positions at the end of the line, and from the front the next threesome was already stepping out to a drumroll.

— When all's said and done, he's a Pole like the rest of us. I mean look at his surname, never mind about his first name.

— If he's a Pole, then I'm not.

— What do you mean, you're not a Pole?

— I mean just what I say, see.

— Then who the hell are you? A Turk? A ruddy Turk?

— I'd rather be a Turk any day than that.

— Pole or no Pole — the bus-stop chipped in — when it comes to it they'll make him into a Sienkiewicz. But first they'll have to stick a few more books under his armpits.

The would-be taxi passenger stood forever motionless, then raised her head and noticed the row of neatly parked Mercedes and Volgas and Tchaikas and Ladas at the far end of the square; she glanced covetously at the row of cars and darted off across the square, banking on easy prey, a small and lonely figure; but two large silhouettes loomed by her side, she gesticulated, pointed toward the cars, waved some coloured banknotes, then headed toward the bus-stop for shelter.

— She was lucky to be let off, if she'd gone any further she'd be no more than a heap of rubble — said the taxi driver, his blue fingers tightening a nut.

The next threesome counted to ten and gave a triple-headed bow to the statue, but its metal head paid no attention and its greenish eyes peered sideways somewhere above the square. The stack of wreaths grew, the wind braided the rib-bons and exotic inscriptions, mingling alphabets and languages across frontiers.

— I'm in such a bad way — someone in the queue was complaining — ever so bad — can you imagine, my TV's broken and I ain't got a clue what's going on, like a moth banging my head against the wall.

— Mmmmm, and there's ever such good things on...

— Well I never, I can't wait to hear...

— Mmmmm, all sorts of stuff like, a guy came from Koscierzyna and did his impersonation of a trumpet, and another guy did a belly dance and tied two feet of thread into two hundred and fifty knots, and there was a guy who played a tune with his nails on his teeth, and a couple that's real popular right now, a brother and sister, duet for two jaws, mmmmmm, and a poetess in overalls from a village near Siedlce sang a pig-song of her own composition, and in the program on carp-breeding the carp at the end said merry Christmas, and then the news bulletin said a lot of passengers had flown into Okecie and couldn't remove their fur coats, mmmmmm, and they turned out to be foxes and the lopsided woman reporter held the mike up to the cage and said good day mr fox, how are you today, what, can't you unbutton yourself, what, he was mute as a fish...mmmmm...

— My old man after all that has connected the TV to the radio and now we watch the box on the radio, and they said there's sex in the sideboard and jangling forks, to which the women said good but only so-so, and oh what a hoot, eight hours the family waited with the stiff, people came from all over Poland, well and then what, no coffin to be had, no coffin for love or money, and then that Walesa stabbed the nation in the back, oh it's a sorry state, a sorry sorry state...

Three heads demurely bowed to the metal boots, yes, yes, yes, they appeared to be reiterating their undying oath, unsure whether the metal figure would altogether trust them.

Then drums rolled once again and the next threesome carried its wreath like a shield against the venomous wind, but the people at the bus-stop did not so much as glance in their direction; they were listening to the woman who woke up with a smile in a corner of the shelter and set eyes on two silent males and was saying to them with gentle persuasion, hey boys, want to have some fun; I've got two daughters, nine and seven, let's have a giggle, I live just across the road, only came out for a breath of fresh air, come on lads, I promise you won't regret it...

The eyes of the previous threesomes rested on the last triplet and its wreath; it was a delegation of Polish youth; it stepped out to the drums, two boys and a girl carrying the wreath, all in chequered trousers; the metal figure on the plinth lured them like a magnet; when they approached, the soldier escorting them walked away; two other soldiers received the coloured wreath from the girl and placed it with some difficulty in the remaining space at the figure's feet; then they stood to attention, and the threesome counted to ten; the girl prompted herself by imperceptibly tapping out the rhythm, then at last the three young heads bowed simultaneously as though to check if they had clean shoes, and the girl's blond hair blew over her forehead and screened her cheeks; the line-up beamed with pride and content at the representatives of Polish youth, and the girl felt the touch of their glances and her cheeks blushed as they stepped lightly past the line-up, borne on the eyes of the onlookers; once they were back in their places, the girl sighed and blew the hair from her cheek, then glanced at her companions and licked her parched lips with the tip of her tongue...

And the band struck again at the sky, and the line-up stood tense as though with cramp and listened earnestly to the song; then order broke, people made a bee-line for the cars, doors slammed and violet lights flashed on the roofs and the cavalcade drove off; the woman running toward the taxi recovered her wits, spotted the cars and began to wave her arm rhythmically, stooping down to the curb; the Mercedes, Volgas, Tchaikas and Ladas sailed by, but she kept on waving her hand; the musicians put away their mouthpieces and shook the saliva from the brass...

And the white caps that had barred the entrance to the square vanished, cars and buses reappeared and in a trice the square was full of people; the scene drifted away like a dream, and only the coloured wreaths lay stacked at the foot of the towering figure...

The taxi driver flung the jack into the car, slammed the lid to no effect, then flapped his hand in resignation and pulled the tail of his jacket from under his duffel and slowly wiped his greasy fingers.

A bus drew up at the stop and those getting off jammed into those getting on; the jittery driver didn't even notice he had lit the filter of his fag and framed his passengers in the wings of his pneumatic doors...

— I could take you in a pinch — the taxi driver said to the woman standing in a daze by the curbside — but only as far as Wola, 'cause I'd make nothing on it; but if we went by Gorczewska Street we could clock up another couple of kilometers, 'cause I've got a cousin who's got the dropsy, that's worth a look in...

The last militiamen and civilians dispersed from the foot of the monument into the crowd.

A man in a short sheepskin jacket appeared at the bus-shelter, extracted a brush from an inside pocket, and on the armoured glass drew large letters that began to shape the word VIC...

The subdued square came alive, people strained their eyes to the point of tears in search of their bus numbers, no one paid attention to the weary provocateur writing on glass. Only the last cop gave him a discreet wink from beneath his visor as he strolled past, gestured faintly with his hand, jerked his chin at the indifferent people and gave a mild shrug of the shoulders...

VICTO...

The Three Kings

The netting, rusty as lichen, bars the assembled people from the garden allotments.

Scorched by the night frost, clusters of limp tulips hang from the net, and a faded icon sways in the gusts of wind.

Behind the netting lonely figures of allotment owners stoop and poke about among last year's overgrowth of weeds; dust rises from clumps of stalks at every touch.

Bent to the ground, they occasionally glance at those the other side of the netting lest anyone try to slip through to their patches. And they ponder the sky and cover the seed-beds with wrapping paper to protect the soil from radioactive dust; they secure the sheets with stones, but the eastern wind delivers its dispatches everywhere.

The slanting walls of glasshouses lie between the people and the town, which resounds today with marching music and bustles like an asiatic bazaar.

The people the other side of the netting stand in a tight huddle; women whisper among themselves and point their fingers and tighten their kerchief knots under their chins; solemn men stand on one side, shielding lit cigarettes in their cupped palms; they exhale an odour of days-old alcohol and insomnia.

— I saw it as sure as I see you.
— You say you saw it?

— That's what I'm telling you. And I can see it now.

— What, in colour?

— In technicolour. Sure as I stand here.

— Sort of rainbow-like?

— What're you driving at? — the woman was perturbed.

— Nothing. Just asking.

— You mean you can see it too?

— No, no, I can't see a thing. I'm only asking if it's rainbow-like.

— Yes, like a rainbow. What d'ya mean? — the woman asks suspiciously. — Can you see something too?

— Not a sausage. And my eyeballs is aching. But nothing doing.

— So now you see.

The people stand rooted in the trampled meadow pitted with mole-hills. The wind inflates the printed papers clinging to the wire.

Behind the wire stretches a row of patches and sheds, botched together from bits of plank, plywood and tar paper.

— Bucher aus Polen — people mouth the inscriptions on the walls.

— That German bicher is good stuff — they say approvingly. It's good stuff, that German bicher, waterproof. Someone brought a crate of it back from a trip. It lasts a good couple of years, too.

— Maybe if it's not burned out by the russki atom — they nod and tilt their heads so as to scrutinize the sheds more professionally.

The allotments are adjacent to the brick wall of the cemetery, above which trees spread out their black boughs. People anxiously search the branches with their eyes — See, where they sort of fork off, that's where it is; there, see, more to the side, by those branches; I can see a blue mantle.

44

Over that shed over there with the veritas on the wall. That's where I can see it.

Far away, three old men stand at a curb, separated from the sidewalk opposite by a lively procession swelling the full width of the roadway; the other side is out of reach, yet they must somehow cross it on their way to the suburbs and the allotments next to the wall of swollen red bricks.

Women in coloured aprons dart along the roadway, their heads immersed in moth ball fumes; hemmed in by a ring of glum men in lacquered boots, they all execute some sort of dance, but the band has not yet struck up and the cavalcade proceeds in a silent void, except for the crackling of puffy breeches and stiff petticoats; — Here come the good folk of Siedlce — the loudspeakers roar overhead — nimble-toed as ever, Siedlce. — Men whose two-day stubble creeps up to their bloodshot eyes sullenly cut capers and spin their scared womenfolk round in a fury.

— Buses aren't working today — the three men say. — We'll never get to the miracle on foot.

— The trams will be coming on later. But we gotta get across. Gotta get to the Vistula.

— Not a chance. They're not letting people through — says the old man with a sun-blackened face.

— How long can the procession last?

— Ages. They go on and on. I must be seeing double, but that's the third time those soldiers have gone by.

— Those women in the aprons have been past once already.

— Not this lot. That was the Lomza contingent. They had aprons too; easy to confuse.

— We'll never make it on time, if this goes on another couple of hours it'll be night.

People stare through the wire mesh at the tree-tops and wait in hope, envying those who have seen and in a feverish exchange of details confirm it was no hallucination.

— A single figure, just by itself.

— Not at all, it was a large, bright-coloured head.

— What head? What are you going on about?

— A head I said. Coloured.

— But a head can't appear by itself.

— Why on earth not?

— Because it can't.

— But it can if it wants. A head can appear by itself if it wants to.

— I tell you it's impossible. It must be full-length.

— But where is it?

— See where the branches form a sort of shelter? It's quite distinct. It's even moving.

— But not there. Your marbles must've come loose.

From the wall of the glasshouses people stream across the meadow; at the sight of the crowd by the wire they quicken their pace, women run, cleaving the air with their bags, and shamefaced smiles fade, full of incredulity. The crowd grows . . .

— Perhaps we might make a dash for it — the old boys think out loud. — When there's an intermission.

— Dash where? We'll be trampled to dust. Not so much as noticed. The procession has eyes only for itself . . . If only . . .

Several sweaty men steal away from the procession clutching a gigantic balloon on a rope; it soars overhead, and the men exchange feverish whispers, wipe their faces and glance on all sides; then one of them accosts the old boys.

— You wouldn't mind holding the balloon, cumrades? Eh? For just a mo? 'Cause we've got business to do . . . And the balloon has to . . . before the stand. You'll take the rope, won't you, cumrades? — a purple man asks with wily hope and

46

at one tug opens the shirt on his swollen neck.

The old men eye one another in panic.

— How long for?

— Only a mo, and...

— And you'll come and collect it? — the old fellow enquires suspiciously.

— I should think so. We signed a chit for it. Have to hand it back after the procession. It's been parading past the tribune for years. At the head, in the middle, a sort of symbol like. In Gierek's day, too, only it went a different route, maybe you remember. Way back in Wieslaw's day even. So you'll take it, eh?

— Just thinking...it won't blow away?

— Not likely. It's half full. Bye-bye then — the man brightens up. — There's nothing like a Pole to give a 'elping 'and.

The old men fumble at the rope, the balloon sways to a wave of military march — Hey mister — the old man calls, but they're cut off from the crowd by a huge wing of red material that flaps about their legs and arms, and when the wind dispels the red haze, the other fellows have gone, vanished into the bowels of the earth.

The ballon hovers docile overhead, the rope flags and they can handle it easily. The balloon slowly revolves and the old boys, laboriously craning their heads, decipher the inscription at its base: *Warm Welcome to the Congress*...

An old woman holds her oil-cloth bag to her left ear to shield it from the needling wind and gazes, eyes teared, at the allotment sheds, the cemetery wall and the trees beyond, and turns back helplessly to the crowd.

— There's no figure there at all, nothing.

— Nothing? — people are bewildered and incredulous.

— Nothing whatsoever. I can't see anything.

— How can there be nothing when they showed it on TV and we saw it? We did.

— TV, oh well, TV. They may've seen a vision. But it's not appearing to me.

— But it's got to — they reassure the disappointed woman.

— Maybe all this atomic wind has blurred it.

The crowd swells, newcomers fidget uneasily — Where's that miracle — they ask. — Over there, above the shed, in the mantle — local men in threadbare jackets with upturned collars patiently explain.

— Now what do we do with this balloon? — the old men ask in dismay. — Those ole boys've gone. Gone with the wind.

— Maybe they'll come back. They said they'd signed...signed a chit...

— They won't come back. They've palmed the balloon off on us.

— I mean we can't take it to the allotments...

— Or get on the tram with it...

— Dump it on someone?

— Who would want it?

They are drowned by the loud menacing words of the song and the shouts of a reporter battling his way through the noise; a disorderly crowd of schoolchildren in trade school caps trails along the street, encircled by a ring of teachers who keep standing on tiptoe and craning their necks to count them; several pupils evade their watchful glances and draw up on the curb; they huddle in apparent consultation, and with nimble fingers they roll up the canvas on the flagstaffs they'd been hoisting; then with the tips of the red-cocooned rods they grope for the sewer manhole and quickly shove them down, and step back onto the sidewalk; the banners disappear down the sewer like floats, and the pupils cower and evade

48

the experienced eye of their tutors.

— Get us Free Europe — one of them says — there may be a bulletin about the cloud...

His mate pulls out a small transistor radio and scans the wave band, catches voices amid the crackles, and they bend their heads over the receiver and hear a woman and a man, and their ravelled words, — There's one solution for loneliness in a woman's life — says the man — it's to become a councillor. A councillor can go to a cafe with her councillor colleague and there's no gossiping. Idiot, that can't be Free Europe — say the disappointed pupils, so the owner of the radio perseveres at the knob and finally gets a report on the procession; a gust of wind tugs at the balloon and the old men dig their fingers into the slippery cord for all they're worth...

— So I saw another figure, slightly to the side. Over that shed, right. Golden rays. Chestnut hair just like yours — and the informant tugs at the hair of the woman standing by her — shoulder-length chestnut hair — she thumps her in the shoulder blades — about so long. With a beard. Sad-faced. Seemed ready for the worst. Seemed to know what was brewing. Oh, and the gold rays, but I told you that already.

— That's more or less what I saw. A full-length figure standing in the branches. Gave me quite a turn, because...

— Oh, I wouldn't swear to it. In the evening I'd see better. But I'm blind as a bat by day. Could be seeing things...

— I can see it moving. This way, that way...

And the inhabitants of the glasshouse stand at the windows with their binoculars aimed alternately at the clump of trees beyond the cemetery wall and at the sky, from which an invisible dust quietly falls.

— Ah, the veterans with the balloon — a woman rushes up to the old men, her coat flying in the wind, and eyes them soberly.

— Come for the balloon? — they hopefully ask. — Here you are. All in one piece.

— Get lost with that balloon — the woman gets excited. — We must make an announcement over the radio, issue hourly communiqués about the peace conference to be convened the day after tomorrow. It must be convened in the Column Hall of Parliament. We must summon a committee immediately to broadcast communiqués every hour about the conference in the Column Hall. I can't get that committee to work.

The old men gaze at the woman in bewilderment and, still holding the rope, tuck their hands behind their backs.

— Yesterday I spoke with a group from Cuba. Very understanding they were. Very sympathetic. The Column Hall of Parliament then. And you'll join the committee. As veterans.

— But the militia'll rout us — one old man hesitantly says.

— So you're afraid of the militia?

— I sure am — the old man says sincerely.

— Well, I'm not. And I'm a woman.

— Because you don't know life, missy. Besides, we haven't got time. We've got to get to Praga. To the allotments.

— Where will it get you, all this running around in circles. There and back. I'm going to the hotels now. There's three hotels in all. I need to find the delegation from Cuba. They'll take part in the peace conference in the Column Hall in Parliament. They promised me. Very decent people. Gave me wholehearted support. And you must sign the declaration.

— I'm not going to sign anything — says the old man, tugging at the rope.

— Well, you might at least have a spot of iodine? — the woman enquires, and without waiting for a reply, she makes a bee-line for a group of steelworkers walking along the road-way in ceremonial costumes.

— My eyes are hanging out and nothing to show for it — says the woman, who turns away disappointedly from the netting, wipes the stains of rust from her fingers and grabs a strand of grey hair of the woman standing next to her.

— My, but you do have light hair. Beautiful — She fingers the head of the motionless woman and pulls back her ears.
— So light and fine. I had a jar of lemon for a couple of years for washing mine, but it fell out all the same. Yours is pretty. The thing is to add spirits to the egg yolk, otherwise it congeals and clogs up the hair. But it's too late now. It'll drop out after that cloud like anything. And we'll all go on the same hearse when we go.

— But I did see it — the woman protests in desperate defence. — Besides, if you believe, you don't have to see, you just believe you see...

— Maybe, maybe not — a pensive voice replies. — Folks these days are suspicious anyway. In the old days they'd lie flat on the ground for a miracle. They don't even know what they want nowadays.

— That's 'cause they can't figure out the sense of things no more — others say soothingly and turn round again in the opposite direction, only to face the brick wall.

— That'll be the thirteenth miracle since the war — one of the old men shouts above the brass band. — The balloon's beginning to make my hands ache.

— Thirteenth. That could bring them bad luck — the second jerks his chin somewhere to the side.

— Thirteenth, that's right. In 'forty-nine it was in Lublin, in 'fifty-seven in Kossak Square in Cracow, in 'fifty-eight in Chelmek... — the third starts counting.

— In 'fifty-nine the tower was alight in Muranow, what

51

had been painted over — says the second.

— In 'sixty-five a girl in Zabludow saw a miracle. So her mother was arrested for spreading false news... — the third expounds.

— 'Seventy-one near Radzymin, 'seventy-four in Piotrkow Kujawski. 'Seventy-five in Wroclaw.

— 'Eighty-one in Olecko.

— 'Eighty-four in Olawa.

— 'Eighty-four in Karczew, too.

— A regular rainfall of miracles over the last few years.

— And what's more, we always used to get there on time. But with this balloon...

A crocodile of white-bonneted nurses proceeds along the highway. The young women glance about them, fidget behind the backs of their friends and break out in nervous, uncontrollable laughter...

And every few steps, at the command of the sister-in-charge, the line alters its pace, gives a hop and a skip as if it had hiccoughs.

A young man sidles up to the three old men, his hand hidden significantly beneath his left armpit; he gives them a professional look-over, then whispers to the one nearest him — Pair of tights for the missis? — and he rustles cellophane beneath his jacket.

— Has anyone seen the miracle? — people pressed, averting weary eyes from the cemetery wall.

— What do you mean, has anyone? Everybody's seen the miracle.

— I've even got a snapshot.

— Then let's see it, madam.

— I haven't got it on me, it's at my sister's. It's in colour.

— Then show us, missis, if that's the case.

— I haven't got it on me, I tell you. It's at my sister's.

Close up you can't tell how to hold it. But from a distance you can. You have to take your hand away to see. All colours. Pink and blue.

— Maybe you're pulling my leg...

Offended, the woman turns away and shrugs her shoulders.

— Say what you like, but a miracle's nothing to scoff at.

A sickly vapour rises above the meadow, people's eyes water. Nauseating kitchen smells come from the concrete wall of the house, as well as the amplified boom of the procession on TV.

The local cop, clutching his satchel in his leather glove, wades through the meadow towards the crowd; the martial music from the procession drives his reluctant pace forward.

And so he reaches the wall of human shoulders, pauses indecisively and opens his mouth to speak, then claps it shut and rushes toward a molehill, burrows with the tip of his boot, crouches, stretches out his hand and straightens up again.

He grasps a dusty pen in his hand, shakes off the lumps of soil, peers round, blows on the ballpoint and positions his left hand to test it, promptly pulls off his leather glove and begins to draw some sprawling characters. He stares at his hand and enunciates, as though reading a bulletin.

— Come on, folks. What's the point of gathering here. Disperse and go home. 'Cause there'll be trouble.

People standing nearby turn round and see the lonely cop facing them; they look at him without fear.

— Come on, folks. There's nothing there. There never was. Not since I came on duty — the constable says hesitantly, his eyes fixed on his left hand. — I mean there's no apparition, nothing...

— Miracles don't appear to sinners — says a voice from the crowd.

— Or the unworthy.

Silence falls, then voices rise again with growing certitude; people exchange astonished looks as though they had made some unexpected discovery.

— Far more useful if you ask me. The worthy don't need it. But the unworthy might be converted...

— Come on, folks, disperse. Don't cause an obstruction. Miracles don't come on tap — he says without conviction, staring at the cluster of trees above the wall...

The old men feel their hands go weak; gusts of wind and music tug the balloon in all directions.

One of them extracts a packet of Populars from his pocket and shoves it toward his companions, and they help themselves with their free hands, then stoop over the slender match flames. Unawares, they let the rope slip from their stiff fingers, and the balloon bounds up into the air, then sideways. A group of small girls with drums strapped to their bellies stop waving their sticks, their wide eyes following its unsteady flight. The wind twists the balloon and hurls it against the banners hoisted on high rods by two railway workers from the junction; the surface rips on the sharp end of one of the rods; it emits a whirring stream of gas and tears the second slogan from the railway workers' hands, *Our Railwaymen Say No to American Nuclear Rockets*, and the balloon tosses madly, causing havoc among the marchers.

Women squeal as they yank their motley dresses; the railwaymen press their caps to their heads and pick up the bent cardboard letters from the asphalt; and the flabby balloon flounders on the pavement like a jellyfish.

Suddenly there's a crowd of youths milling about the three terrified old men, hemming them in, grabbing them tight by the arms; several bellicose commands and sentence fragments assail them: disruption of proceedings, sabotage of ceremony;

but they can't understand what has happened and look round helplessly and don't know why they are being frog-marched towards a grey police van.

— We must get to the allotments . . . — one of them tries to say, then falls silent.

— You'll be getting your allotments — they hear a jeering voice. — Everybody'll get their allotment.

And when they stand outside the open door of the van and look up, they start to mention that the step is too high, but all they hear is the snap of words — Hey, you three kings, hop into the disco . . .

Chain of Pure Hearts

The pair of them stood silently facing each other; not a word; then they hunched, squatted and began simultaneously to retreat, jostling people indifferently; they looked like two dwarfs readying for a duel, and the red folds they were unfurling over the ground grew longer and longer between them till they couldn't take half a step more on this leash, so they straightened up; they held the ends of the material, peered at the letters in yellow glitter, and attempted to flick off the remnants of old slogans, but the glue gave way and the slogan surged overhead for a moment; they jerked their heads in amazement and even had time to read it; *Come Sun, Come Rain, Come Join the Chain*; the wind struck and the letters gyrated like little albatrosses; the layout began to disintegrate; first the slogan lost its meaning, then the words; the wind whipped up again and carried the loose letters and dashed them against the black bosom of the stone giantess propping her shoulders against the wall of the Palace of Culture.

The pair of them observed the flight of the slogan, letters, words and then as the white scraps scattered on the stone lady's lap and feet they shrugged their shoulders, turned about toward the van, selected the next roll of cloth and again started moving backwards on their haunches, as though they were hunting for fag-ends among the cracks of the granite flagstones; a white slogan bloomed: *Don't Miss the Boat,*

Go and Vote; they mouthed syllables amid the scraping and clatter of numerous feet, shrugged their shoulders, wound the material up, carried it back to the van, found another roll and without a word began walking backwards in the shadow of Stalin's pyramid.

People were assembling in the square, watching the television team entangle itself in cables, the lackadaisical reporters and cameramen with their equipment, a small purple man in a cyclist's cap cramming words into a mike; he stood in an open car, and tense assistants busied over him as they recorded his speech; he kept straying from the mike and signalling; the assistants would rewind the tape and play it back; he listened keenly, turned more and more purple, and grabbed back the mike, glancing at a wad of index cards — A magnificent concern, integration, let us defend, the idea of love, we shall be the first in our country, to be victorious, love, love, dearly beloved, for we'll always be together, elderly, let's join hands young and old alike, chain, to love, love, let's all clasp hands and we shall stand, the way of truth, our chain shall unite the land, our honesty sincerity success joy happiness, my, our, we'll be together, our common road, understanding, common life, ours, to love, love, chain, the whole country, to embrace, understanding, to embrace, join hands, everyone, everyone, to love — and he heard these words again, pressing the mike to his cyclist's cap, and in the increasing hubbub the pair of them unfurled the next slogan and read it with cocked heads and shrugged their shoulders: *The Chain Belongs to All of Us, Without It You're Not One of Us*.

The first drops of rain cut through the air and died in a hiss on the cracked flagstones; a reporter took a plastic bag from under his arm, removed two sandwiches from it, stuffed the bread into his pocket and with an awkward movement

of one hand attempted to pull the bag over his head to protect his hair; scratching his skull, he sauntered up to a group
of people standing quietly to the side clasping hands.

— The chain? Are you the chain? — he casually asked.

— The chain of pure hearts! — they replied, and he looked
like a conductor as he caught voices from various angles with
deft movements of the mike.

— We've waited a long time for an initiative of this sort.
And now the chain has been launched at last, it will unite
us from the mountains to the sea, it will be a milestone on
the way to national conciliation, a powerful protest against
the cosmic spiral of cowboy... — and the reporter nodded
his head in time and chewed his rain-sodden bread, and when
he switched off the mike, the others let go their hands and
clustered round him. — Will it be on the radio, will it be
broadcast? I should say it will — he replied, munching his
bread. A savvy sort of girl said — You're an old hand at
this, aren't you? — and he winked and shrugged as the mike
began again to catch the milling throng — The thought at
once occurred to me, it did, that if all of us in this country
were to unite like one man and raise hands, it would be a
great cause, well, I don't know, but a great cause, if all thirty-
six million of us linked up and showed how many of us there
really are...

— Pushing thirty-seven million now... — someone interjected from the side. — The latest statistics...

— Well thirty-seven then; it'll be a great cause!

— Attention! — shouted the little man in the cyclist's cap
— attention! We're starting now! We're joining hands from
the mountains to the sea! Up and down the country, far and
wide! I am with you!

People began to retreat in unaccountable panic, but it was
too late, for hands had already clenched in tight grips, and

the assistants of the man who was directing every movement over the loudspeaker stepped out into the crowd and steered people into line and in their outstretched arms they caught giggly women trying to abscond, and the chain grew longer and it emerged from the ashen shadow of the palace and bisected the vast square; the pair of them walked slowly backwards unfurling the cloth, checked the slogan, shrugged their shoulders: *Don't Wait to Be Asked Again, Come and Join Our Pure Heart Chain*; and on the side the cameraman froze in a catatonic pose as he recorded an interview; words impressed the passive tape — Our chain alas lacks many, and here I'd like to take the opportunity; the lack of links, but I tell you it can all be put right; a man who no longer feels he's one of us, proof of expiation, admit to errors; one could admit to having erred and overshot the mark, but that's the only road, expiation, it has already, as it were, has been recognized, so to speak, and so to, truth, an attempt, this resentment, this feeling, and now they've exploited, renounced citizenship; it's complex; they left on impulse, it's not easy to tackle; on the one hand they were refused, we know instances of, and so forth, they came back and confessed, not just a question of valid passports; what reasons, what excuses; if he still wants a passport come and say, come and explain and appeal, always appeal — and the chain was growing, snaking already round the corner of the store.

Eager reporters followed the line of people and prodded them with their mikes; the raindrops lashed them even as they averted their faces, but no one had the guts to desert the chain; the wardens circulated through the streets and rounded up passers-by; where, where, which way, join the chain, they urged the recalcitrant; the chain bulged and was now skirting the bank; with an automatic pistol slung over his shoulder, a guard stood like a post on the stone steps, muttering monotonously in his beard — Dollars, dollars, anyone got any hard currency to sell — the chain grabbed and swallowed him before he had time to realize he was already one of the links; on one side a sinewy woman gripped him in her chapped palm, on the other a boy with a willow-green topknot; the guard bridled and tugged away in a bid to reach for his pistol, but he was in no state to make a move.

— And what does the chain mean to you? — the reporter cried. — What do these pure hearts mean to you? — he jabbed the man standing nearest with his mike. Like one roused from a trance, he shook himself and answered in a quiet voice — Basically I'm for porn. Specially when several knock up one woman, get me? Though I don't fancy woman with dog...

And his neighbour, while squeezing his hand in her whitened fingers, protested violently; her cheeks went puce and she choked, then controlled her coughing — Oh no, dearie, society's not up to it. It's nauseating. Not even stimulating. In the lower orders it's popular for one woman and two...

— Why? — the man said in a suppressed voice. — When that's what she wants? In that case lay her, that's what I say — and he was seized by a paroxysm of thinnish laughter, but the reporter had long since moved on.

The chain now ran along the alleys, then straightened out in a wide avenue; the little man in the cyclist's cap stood in the open car with his mike, roaring over the loudspeaker to the chain, turning dangerously purple — News has reached us that the chain from the southeast is getting ever closer; let us unite midway and when we unite let's raise our hands aloft for joy; let's give it a trial run: hands up — he bellowed over the loudspeaker. The chain tensed but its hands compliantly ascended and froze in the air. Soon it began to droop, for it was laden with nets and bright bags from foreign supermarkets. An emaciated blond youth in a jacket with an upturned collar alone had his hands free; gripping his leather bag between his teeth for convenience, he leaned forward from the rank; his tongue lisped against the artificial leather — My pure heart bearth gifth for the Party — and he craned his neck perilously forward, but no microphone succeeded in capturing his voice. — That boss — someone said grudgingly as the car and loudspeaker moved away — that chain boss, he knows what makes a duck quack all right; for every bod he rounds up, he gets ten groszy cash in hand. So do your sums, mister — and he jerked his head violently as though to resist suffocation — for ten he gets one zlot, right? Ten zlots for a hundred. A hundred for a thousand. A thousand for ten thousand. And Bob's your uncle, enuf for half a litre. No work involved.

— He'll get a medal for the chain. And a bonus for the medal — someone chipped in.

— You bet. Specially as it's all anti-subversion — the man jerked his head — Must be a medal. For a start there's the half litre. When he rounds up twenty thousand, there's two half-litres. Enuf! He won't round up thirty thousand, but he can have a good binge all the same. Son of a bitch! — the man tossed his head about in a rage till ripples went down the chain.

The head of the chain had moved far away, passing a gate where an old man stood staring at the sky, spitting out words that ricocheted; from the corner of his eye he saw the chain approaching and shouted all the louder as though he hoped to be heard — Lookie folks, I've had sixty-five years slog and grind from dawn to night and what, bus tickets eighteen a ride; from dawn to night; slog and grind, slog away

62

greyhead, you stupid old greyhead — and he pummelled his forehead with his fists and stamped. The chain grabbed his hands as though to spare his head, took him in noiselessly and careered down the street.

A car drew up alongside the chain and out jumped a cameraman and some other fellow who wanted to latch on. The cameraman focused his lens, but there was an outcry and the man hesitated — Blumin' cheek, you weren't standing here, now were you, confess; and the man jumped back into the car, the cameraman followed suit and off they drove.

The chain wound round a statue; iron figures in tin coats ready to shoot from antiquated rifles huddled on the plinth; all stared through steely eyes in one direction and in that direction the chain expanded and slowly approached the Monopol shop; a woman drenched to the skin stood in front of the shop, and two men held a banner with a flowery inscription above her head: *You Don't Need Alcohol to Have a Fun Time*; another man stood swaying in front of them shouting — Bravo, bravo — he stifled his hiccoughs and laughed, and rain mingled with the tears on his cheeks — Bravo; it's three months since I came off the booze, and I've only got nine months to go before I'm awarded a small coronation sword; only nine more months to go; that sword's the brainchild of the DT colleagues in our anti-alcohol group and they've made it so that two years off the bottle gets you a larger sword, and three years to an even larger one; that big, big as a chicken — and he spread out his hands to demonstrate the size of the sword; that's just what the crowd was waiting for, and it scooped him up from outside the Monopol shop; a man leaped out of the doorway squeaking; the squeak issued from under his jacket, and he spoke feverishly, adjusting his collar and looking helplessly round; only a trampled banner with the flowery message separated him from the people in

63

the chain, *You Don't Need Alcohol to Have a Fun Time*; and some rapt journalist was noting the fervent words of a girl in his soggy notebook — For me the chain means everything and from this time on I'm going to be a completely different person, because I have seen that I'm not alone, that we are legion — the man's eyes lit up; he took the journalist gently by the elbow and led him into the doorway; the journalist walked instinctively, paying no heed and jotting down the last words — I love the chain — and the damaged shortwave transmitter gave a soft squeal...

A woman in the chain glanced at her neighbour and squeezed his fingers meaningfully; he stooped towards her and started humming in a flat tenor — No one knows just how wonderful you are — and she passed her tongue over her lips and whispered — You're a cute little nightingale...

— We can always find a way — her neighbour resumed, bowing his head, but at that moment a car came roaring by — Hands up for a trial run; the northeast has crossed over the Vistula — and the cyclist's coloured cap flashed past; the couple's hands rose submissively, and they turned away from each other like strangers.

— Is your sector for or against? — a frozen pedestrian enquired in sudden interest, clapping his wet beret against his knees like a Cossack dancer.

— Depends... — uncertain voices replied.

— What I mean is... For the Party or against?

— It varies...

— Because the sector in the passage there's shouting Lech, Lech, and one fellow's singing *I've flushed my Socialist Youth badge down the bog*, and round the corner they're crying long live the second stage of the economic reform and we go along with PRON all the way. In the square they're singing religious stuff... Well?

— Yes and no...

— Not really...'Cause I don't know... Where'm I to join?

— And you mister...I meantersay...

— You tell first...

— It varies...I've joined the chain because my wife ditched me for another guy. And it hurts.

— I know it hurts — the passer-by replied. — What's more it's meant to...

— You just go up to the front and ask there. They'll tell you. 'Cause we...what've we... We were told to stand here, that's why. Mind you, there might be a flash on the box...a treat for the kids. The TV's passed by once this way but they didn't film us. Next time maybe. How can we know what the chain really...

— They say it's to build bridges...to be socially-minded...

The far end of the chain distended in zigzags, warily sidestepping the puddles churned up by the wheels of a passing car; a purple face flashed by in the rain, booming from the car roof — My heart is pure, is yours? Southwest getting close! Hands aloft! Joy! Joy!

A lacework of hands poised in mid-air...

Hard by the church a subdued queue was washed down by the rain; women whispered cautiously among themselves — I'm standing in for my hubby as he couldn't...a perfectly valid excuse...

— Standing in...

— 'Cause my hubby couldn't...actually he's drunk, but perhaps he'll cure him from a distance, that miracle-healer...

— Can't do it, not from a distance — the women started whispering. — His powers don't reach that far.

— He must lay his hands in person...

65

— He doesn't cure drunkenness.

— He cures everything... Here's my husband's ticket...

— How can he heal him? Where's he to lay his hands? On his throat?

— I suppose so... Where else?

— What sort of an illness is it if a man drinks? It's worse when he don't work. Then he's not a man. Can't call him a man, not if he don't work. He's not a man. I'm not saying he's a child. But he has to drink, 'cause otherwise he won't work...

The chain was getting closer and the women lining up outside the healer's now noticed it and shuffled uneasily and craned forward, shielding their watery eyes with their palms — What is it, what is it? — the women murmured. — What d'ya mean? I guess it's a method of linking hands to create a current and the current passes through and cures everything; they say it's better than laying on of hands when a current like that strikes; what d'ya mean better, laying on of hands is far the best; they say the current's better; I've had the current four times; but why've they come barging along here with that current of theirs; they can go back where they came from; it's obvious why; to have a choice of cure; there's two ways of looking at it; I'm not budging, I've got me ticket for laying on of hands, I'm not going to waste me ticket; then you stay put, no one's forcing you, see; say what you like, a current's a current — and individual silhouettes start to slip away from the line of women and head toward the chain, with hands outstretched...

— North's approaching! North's getting closer every minute! Latest news, the North is at the city gates! — the loudspeaker howled from the car roof, and bloodshot eyes closely assessed the row of people. — Today we'll join the whole country in a chain! Tomorrow we'll unite the entire

66

globe! Now for a trial run! Hands up! — and hands rose and gleamed like bronze in the rain. And the chain turned beyond the receding car and overtook the women at the sacristy door.

— What'll the chain change deep down in your life? What? — the reporter quizzed, prodding her expansive breasts with the mike, while the woman attempted to collect her thoughts; she bit her lips, and her neighbour poked his head from between raised shoulders and whispered in a pained voice — This system has its merits...

The lady reporter charged up and down the ranks — What system, what merits — voices on either side soared above the raised hands — what, which system, what merits, that man asked; now what was it you said about the merits of the system; just what is it you have it mind; what did I say? there we go; but who said, say what you like the system has its merits; I said nothing of the sort; you must've dreamed it madam, sure you're feeling all right? — and the man attempted to lower his hands as though to shield himself, but was unable to move; the chain overhead was so strong that it lifted his feet momentarily off the ground.

And people exchanged uncertain glances, warily poking their heads beyond the pure hearts chain — It won't come off with the menfolk; I ask you, how could it, where's their sense; how, where...

— Without'em it'll be another mighty flop, I'm telling you; one great awful mighty flop, oh-h-h — the woman trying to answer the reporter's question began to lament.

— Our chain'll get us going! Our chain'll get the country going again! — words from the distant loudspeaker rattled against the massive house walls.

— What's that? What chain? — someone in the line was intrigued.

— Us. We're the chain, the chain is us. You're the chain too.

— What, me?

— Then whataya standing there for?

— We'll know in good time. They'll end up telling us what. Issue some communiqués... I'll give you chain, you scum — and the man lunged at his neighbour, but the chain didn't flinch.

A vanload of militiamen now entered the street and upon sighting the chain of pure hearts, the driver instinctively slowed down; keen eyes glimmered behind the panes but quickly dimmed as the van accelerated; its blue pulsating light flailed the faces of those standing there and a dark streak focused on them just one moment more, then streamed away noiselessly.

Both ends of the chain are growing, even though the wardens are nowhere to be seen and the rain carries darkness above the roofs; the last cameraman and reporter jump into the car and set off; they drive past a wall of people, and the reporter sits comfy in the shadow muttering to himself — It's like drawing a sickle out of an arse, that chain...

The ends of the chain progress at their own pace and prowl between the houses; rare passers-by link on — I'm sort of for this chain, though I can't say how I feel about things — confides a subdued voice, then falls silent...

Suddenly one end of the chain passes beyond the bend in the wall and freezes in its tracks as it comes face to face with the other end, which has come the wrong way, and both ends look at one other, bewildered; they are separated by no more than a narrow strip of lawn, but by now the street is empty and the chain goes limp; each end eyes the other; — They were meant to be across the Vistula long ago; or maybe we were meant to... — and a voice crescendos — Trial run! hands up! hands up! — the open car with the little man in the cyclist's cap emerges from round the bend, and when he sees both ends of the chain, he turns frantically white, stupefied to silence; the car speeds past in a veil of watery dust and mist as the man thumps his fists against the cabin, then whips his cap from his head, chucks it to the ground and runs it over . . .

As the car vanishes for good in the dark, a hoarse bellowing blares from the loudspeaker on the roof — Not that way, ca-a-nt! Not that way!

A Sense of

High up, as far as a man can reach: KOR = Jews! And just below: You're a Jew too, you Jew!

They were old graffiti, scratched with a sharp implement on the blackened wall of the elevator; no longer erasable.

The man shifted as he stared in amazement at the letters and moved his fingers along the groove, then succumbed, pulled out a pen and pressed with his thumb; but the spring shot up like a spark; shadows suddenly flapped desperately overhead and he felt a knock in the air, and panic; raising his head, he saw a scared pigeon battling beneath the ceiling till finally it clung to the metal contraption that made it impossible to steal the light bulb, and the shadows of its wings froze; the man gasped for air and, when he recovered, extracted a bottle from under his trouser belt, flicked off the stopper, raised it to his mouth and drank, looking sideways at the pigeon that hung bat-like beneath the bulb.

The man slowly aimed his finger at the button and pressed it without withdrawing his hand; the elevator set off in violent downward jolts; again he raised the bottle, but missed the mark and vodka spilled over his chest.

So he drew his stomach in deep and began to tuck the stopperless bottle behind his belt when some slips of paper and photographs fluttered down his loose trouser leg and splayed at his feet like a pack of cards; some of the photos were turned picture side up; others, shiny white, were scrawled over with notes; at his feet lay the picture of a factory in a forest, barricaded by an open-work concrete fence, the other side of which pipes sprawled and bulged at one end like tank barrels, a railway siding with a row of trucks and blurred human figures holding flashlights in the dark, solemn people grouped round a priest at a table; the man moved his leg and unwittingly trod on a small snapshot of two withered women standing in the snow above a black stain that looked like the remains of dried blood; with a whine the elevator plummeted down the shaft.

Silence and mist covered the vast square; its houses lay in decay, unreal as a stage backcloth: jutting balconies stacked with discarded objects, broken chairs, faded children's toys, scraps of refuse, dusty jars and bottles, saucepans with holes and cracked enamel, voiceless TV boxes, old-fashioned chandeliers, rotting picture frames, rusty bikes, strung-up bundles of old newspapers.

The wind occasionally whipped up the mist, driving along plastic yoghurt containers that rattled like Purim mills...

A weathered scrap of cardboard hung in the window of a closed-down kiosk with the words, Special Offer: Buy a calendar with your dreambook and receive a free gift poster commemorating the 300th anniversary of the Relief of Vienna.

These houses were alien here, built provisionally, as though the old proprietors of other apartments in no longer existing houses would soon return and bring the neighbourhood to life.

Several leafless trees stood still in the square, and the pile of black snow turned to bone beneath them, like charnel ice.

The sparse weeds failed to cover the trampled earth, from which rusty jar-tops and fragments of glass protruded; again the mists turned about bearing heavy scraps of newspaper and stifled guttural cries and the shrill of a whistle.

The man stood swaying outside the building, looking, faltering, pressing his eyelids — It's so dark, is there an eclipse today? Maybe the eclipse's today, the ecl. . .

— Mister. What eclipse? — he heard a voice and removed his fingers from his swollen eyelids and blinked, but no image emerged out of the mist opaque as a bladder. — That's no eclipse. There was a better one yesterday. It's just a rum sort of mist today. It sticks to you. Stifles you. Like it always does.

— For a split second I couldn't see — the man said. — I thought there might be an eclipse today. . .

— Not today there's no eclipse. It's Women's Day today. There was even a pep-talk on the radio this morning telling us to love our womenfolk today. They have their feast day too. It's not an eclipse. It's the wrong date. But there was a better one yesterday. Or the day before. Nothing doing. I'm here. And you're facing the other way.

And the man spun round, strained his bloodshot eyes and saw an old man standing there.

— So that's where you are — he said. — Because I was beginning to think I was talking to myself. And where's Gensia?

— What Gensia?

— Gensia Street. Where is Gensia Street? I can't seem to find it.

— What Gensia? There's no such street. You've come on a wild goose chase. . .

— What do you mean, no such street? It's here on the map.

— It may've been once. But how long ago? Anyway it's all gone. Anielewicz's where Gensia used to be. I remember Gensia. Doesn't exist now. It's gone.

— So where's Gensiowka?

— What Gensiowka...

— The prison in Gensia Street. Gensiowka. I'm looking for Gensiowka. I know someone there. Political. In Gensiowka. It must be documented.

— There's no Gensiowka. It's gone. Way back in Gomulka's day. How can you know someone there if it doesn't exist. It's gone. I just remember the demolition and how those idiots made a beeline for the walls. With pickaxes. Spades. You name it. Crowbars. Grubbing for the gold left by the Jews. Greedy for what the Jews had left. And where of all places? In prison. Thought it was walled up. Ignorant deluded lot. They saw Jewish gold everywhere. In prison walls. You name it. Chisels. Exhaust pipes. Bare nails. There's stupidity for you, eh? Like Mongols. Like locusts. You've got into a right twist with that Gensiowka of yours, 'cause I know every inch of this place. I'm applying for the keeper's job.

— I went up in the elevator — the man said — to see the view from the top floor. 'Cause I can't find it. But there're no windows on the stairway. So I came down again and I'm still looking. Melted into thin air, that Gensiowka. Someone I know's inside.

— It's gone, mister. Everything here's gone. This is the ghetto. All that remains of Gensiowka is this naked square. Here. See? Here. Where we're standing. There was a pit where this knoll is now. A dark cell. A pit. Here. I know every inch. This square. You can't see it now because of the mist. Know what I mean?

— Then perhaps he's not inside. Only playing. That rings a bell. I could've got it wrong. If he's not inside he might be playing. Playing in Gensiowka. That should be documented too.

— It's all the ghetto here. Sometimes the ground spits up

74

a brick. Like from a cellar. Those bricks come crawling out of the earth.

— Yeah, I got it muddled. He plays here. The politicals play football here once a week. The prisoners. I got it wrong. Because either he's inside, or he's playing. So first I thought he was inside. Now I remember in fact he's playing. Not inside.

— Some rascals were kicking a ball around here. Old men. And they're still at it. Politicals, you say. What d'ya mean? There's only bones and ashes under the turf. I thought they must be hooligans. Strange that someone wants them to be playing football here. Acting on orders, like. But for politicals to play football? In a cemetery? Mind you, it used to be Jewish. So it's nobody's. So everybody makes a grab. Are you sure?

— They play here. Once a week. I keep records.

— I even thought of chasing them off — the old man said. — Only I was afraid they'd sack me on the spot. But I will in due course. When I take over as keeper. 'Cause at present I got no right to interfere. This area's called Amusement Park Square. There's an information board. Regulations. Not to throw litter. No cycling. There's something about ponds in the regulations, but it's been painted over. Where's there a pond here? Not to litter the ponds. There's never been a pond here. So they painted over the ponds. All under the heading amusement park square. Politicals you say. And where we're standing there was a sewer manhole during the Jewish uprising. Here. A manhole. They were political too. Yes or no? It looks to me that as a nation we've had it for good and all. And stinking crazy beyond hope. I mean. From every point of. Not long ago some folks drove up here in a Polonez. I know everything. They jumped out and started throwing things at the memorial.

See the streamers hanging there. No one cleans up. It was eggs, only you can't see it in this mist. The old woman just barely dragging her feet, leaning on that boy. His neck is bruised. Father carrying the child. His hands are bruised. And that's the way they go to Stawki, to the train. That's where they loaded them, where the filling station is. What's the politics behind it all. To come bumbling along with a filling station in Deportation Square? That's politics for you. But to come bumbling along and play football on the ruins? Just as well the mist hides it all. When I get the job, I'll chase 'em all off, I will. Only how to get the job? 'Cause the secretary took offence and put me down as blind on my identity card. What do they mean, blind? I'm trying for the keeper's job, but they keep saying how can I be a keeper when I'm blind. So I tell 'em and show 'em I can see. They say that on my identity card I'm blind. Blind, me? They tell me to change my card. But how can I change my card when I'm already registered as blind. That blindness is going to stick to me, they'll stamp it in my next card too. And I can see everything. Over there on the other side there's a glass case. Youth festival. And there's photos. A tug-o'-war. Some have completely curled up at the edges. The tug-o'-war's still OK. You can't see it from here, but I know. You won't be able to see, but I can. Dusty photos. In the middle of the square there's a sandpit for kiddiwinks. Faced with old bricks. From the ghetto. That's also politics for you. If I got that keeper's job, I could clear up a few things around here. Though mind you, I'm scared. Might get the sack. That there was the tram route before the war. Okolna line.

— It will all have to be documented — the man muttered as he thoughtlessly touched his stomach; he came sharply to his senses, grabbed his trousers in his fist and began to fumble and to shove his palms under his belt . . . He stiffened and whispered — My documents've been stolen...disappeared. Photos. Notes. Everything. All that travelling. Train journeys. Where haven't I been! Just came back from a place where they built blocks in the 'fifties in the shape of Stalin's name. But you could only see it from the air. It was only later, when they built annexes, that the word vanished. I had it all in a file. I found a factory in a forest and I'm sure it's for armaments, 'cause why else would it be in a forest; I had a photo...

The photo left behind in the elevator showed a factory in a forest, circled by a concrete fence, and with sprawling pipes; patches of melting snow turned dark, revealing a garbage-heap of medicine packings left over from the autumn railway robbery; a siren sounded for break, the broadcasting system started up, and jaunty music swamped the square; when it broke off, voices of the staff could be heard, recorded at the end of a long-forgotten year, but the announcer had no other recordings — How has this last year been? Was there anything special? If it's names you're after, I'm not mentioning anyone; no, no, it's not names we want, just was there anything special; special, no; then perhaps something different; nothing different; then maybe some important day; important, the only important day will be the first day in the New Year, I mean tomorrow...; workers' protest basically justified — another voice spoke up — basically a small group exploited class dissatisfaction; yes, yes, but was there anything different about the year that's ending; different, no; then maybe something special; special, well, we had that plurals in the trade union; but was anything different for you; not one iota; work is basically stultifying, just running round the old tread-mill; and what would you wish for, madam, in this year coming hard on us; nothing for me personally, but I can't speak for others. — Then the courtyard was flooded with lively music, which startled a flock of birds that fluttered over the gate inscribed with the words in English, *Long Live Peace* . . .

The watery mist above the square revealed the rubble of the building. The grey windows on the first floor were plastered over with crisscross strips of paper. Next to the dry cleaners, workmen had abandoned their excavation half-finished; soil remained heaped above the trench along with swollen crumbs of amber bricks and the shreds of disused milk canisters that had once secreted important papers.

A yell rent the cloak of mist, *goal, goal,* then shouting, and a dull whistle.

— Did you hear that? — the old man said. Scoring goals. Confound 'em. It's in the regulations in black and white that visitors to the park and the greens are forbidden to use cycles or other vehicles, to destroy the architecture or park facilities, or dig pits. Now they're playing football. Scoring goals. There's no paragraph in the regulations for that. Not even under common sense.

But the man was not listening, he was patting his stomach just to make sure — See, friend, I didn't even notice them steal the stuff; all my work lost in a jiff; I had everything on file; photos; people on a loading platform; train carriages; checking what goes to the East in those wagons, at night; quite a dab hand at photography . . .

And the flashlights on the platform blinked; numerous figures stooped in the dark; people with cold-stiff fingers dug out from the snow lumps of coal dropped from the trucks while unloading during the day; bags and briefcases bulged, hands weighed every stone and clump of snow — Go on, scoop up all you can, man; how much can you dig away like that — a figure straightens up, and the light is switched off to spare the batteries. — When I was picking up coal once during the German occupation, the railway sentry fired a shot at me and missed, which is why I'm still at it now; otherwise I'd have long since bitten the dust — and the light flashed again, and fingers begin to sift the snow...

— Yes, yes. Folks used to roll up when that lot was playing, wanting to join in — the old man said. — But it was no go. They had their own teams and wouldn't let 'em join in. And they always played with a sort of a frenzy, kicking so hard, yessir, that their legs groaned.

And the owner of a car stepped slowly backwards on the lawn and cocked his head to examine the car, then lunged forward, pulled out a rag and rubbed away some stains with a blob of foam, and shifted backwards again with his head to one side. — There's a guy here that's always washing his car; I'd chase him away for that, yessir, but I'm too scared; might get sacked... Washing his car...

The man stooped to insert his hand knee-high up his trouser-leg, then straightened up with a resigned air.

— And the cosy chat with the priest? What? — he cried, striking his forehead with the palm of his hand.

The room in the photograph was squalid, scantly furnished, the rickety table covered in oil-cloth; a priest sat at the table, a surpliced acolyte crouched behind his back, and a family stood solemnly around him; the father of the family lay on a pallet at the back of the room, propped on his elbow.

And he broke into a hoarse cough, then tried to raise himself and sit up, but immediately fell back on his elbow; all he could do was shout through his coughing and wag his finger at the people by the table.

— The missis drinks! The daughter drinks! Son-in-law drinks! Grand-daughter drinks! I'm the only one in the family that doesn't drink!... They all drink!

— And who was it went to a brothel in Warsaw? Even before the war? — the old woman bellowed from the table.

79

— Who?

— But I paid! — the old boy wheezed.

— If you paid, it's in order — the priest laughed to himself and scooped an envelope up from the table.

— I pay for my own booze — the son-in-law shouted arrogantly.

— If it's your money, it's no sin — the priest mumbled, then rose and made for the door, pushing the absent-minded acolyte before him. No sooner in the hall he opened the envelope, had a quick look and handed it to the acolyte — Enter it on the chart, but do get it right; one always must check, one always must check in case they've stuffed the envelope with newspaper . . .

The stamping of feet could be heard through the thick mist, and the hoarse breathing of the football players, and cries of pain.

— Fancy a drop? — the man asked.

— I don't drink — the old man said as he ran his hand over the brown stones facing the sewer manhole — 'Cause I can't. If I could, I wouldn't say no. — And he bent over the inscription, mouthing the words.

— All fuckin' useless — he said. — But if they'd survived, they'd have had another twenty-five years to go to the anniversary. And another deportation. From the Gdansk station to Vienna. It's not far. Just beyond Deportation Square. It all came to an end in one spot. Like it was a question of politics. Or mere convenience. But nowadays? Where's the convenience? What's the politics? Why keep tormenting them? Torment the living. Torment the dead. They even torment the memorial. A pile of bricks. What sort of politics is that? Where's the sense? All fuckin' useless. Fuckin' useless. There's nobody, not even to weep.

But the man was not listening, only staring at the round

manhole and frowning — To have lost that file, he brooded, all those documents... — The manhole opens and out they come, for they were there...

— What? — asked the old man.

— No. Nothing. It's lost for good. It can't be compiled again. All filed away you know where. I had a photo of a woman at the spot of the tragedy. Blood on the snow. It was in someone's interest for it not to see the light of day.

The photo he had trampled in the elevator showed the shadowy silhouettes of two women standing in the snow; between them a black stain like dried blood; the express flew past — It must be six, around six or seven; must be between six and seven; it flew past just a second ago.

— The way we work, no clock, no time — the woman said.

— So the two of them drank and drank with nothing to eat, then one fell asleep, so for a bite the other cut out a piece of his buttock with his penknife, what a surprise when he wakes up and finds a snack, and he bled away and they found him stiff, just here, he was dead in no time; the two of them were drinking in the bushes here, and the blood vanished completely.

— Maybe he froze? 'Cause there's not much blood.

— Maybe, maybe he did. But with a penknife they said, for a snack. As a surprise. Where's the sense?

The old man was listening to the sound of the football match; he cupped his hand to his ear and raised his head high like a blind man.

— All that trouble for nothing. And who'll believe it all now? — the man said, he pulled in his stomach, reached inside his trouser belt for the bottle. He thrust back his head, as though listening to the match like the old man, then took a swig and spoke bitterly — To get the hell out of here at last, emigrate as far away as possible; enough of this struggle, how much can a man take; I'd like to be a bootblack in New York, in a street with theatres, and shine the shoes of actors and producers and spend all my dough on going to the theatre and see more and more plays and get to know the different actors and shine their shoes and whisper something to each of them; try entering the stage from a different angle; keep that frown for later, more expression there, and in time it will be clear that my every remark has its impact, that he's polishing and perfecting his style, and over the years I become the best shineman in New York, and the actors and producers flock to me, for everything I say turns true, all the theatres need me, their success depends on me and I pull all the strings, and that's when I choose to die and everyone sees what a void I've left and they can't do a thing without me and they look for me and all those celebrity actors and producers come at last to the shabby little room where I lived and in that shabby little room they find everything I was most attached to all those years and all they see is my copy of *Pan Tadeusz* and a handful of native soil . . .* What's left for me to do here? You simply can't make a move. I've already done my bit. The young can get on with it now. It's their turn.

— Yeah, yeah — the old man said. — And when they had the bright idea of building a filling station in Deportation Square, they forgot to make underground tanks. And the first loads went straight into the earth. Thousands of litres. That's their policy for you: National Petroleum Umschlagplatz.**

* Poland's national epic, by Adam Mickiewicz, 1834.

** The railway sidings in Warsaw from which Jews were herded off to Treblinka and other Nazi concentration camps. (Translator's notes)

— I'm not going to stick my neck out any longer — the man said, pulling in his belly and reaching beneath his belt.

— That thirty-storey block you can see from everywhere, they've been building it for the last twenty-five years and they can't get it finished — the old man said. Because they built it on the site of a synagogue. And the rabbi cursed it. He did, I tell you.

— When I still had a wife, my wife always used to say it's like fighting windmills — the man reflected. — That no one will appreciate the effort. And now? Now that I'm empty-handed?

The wind parted the mist. The men had finished their game and stood apart, bending down as though looking for something, heavily gasping for air.

— Seem to have stopped playing — the old man strained to listen. — At one time they didn't even want to play, refused in fact, 'cause the whole pitch was mucked up and the local riffraff brought their dogs onto the pitch; how can you play in a cesspit? That was when someone lit a fire under the memorial plaque on Anielewicz's bunker. The bunker's just there; in winter, mothers take their children tobogganing there and the kids come sailing down from the bunker; the heat from the fire cracked the stone . . . They didn't fancy playing then, oh no . . .

— Can't you chase them away?

— Beg your pardon?

— Couldn't you get a stick? And chase them away? Give them a thrashing?

— Wouldn't mind chasing 'em. But I haven't got permission. And no way to get it, 'cause the secretary took offence and put me down as blind . . .

— Forget about permission. Next time they play you could give them a sound walloping, the opposition, and I'd take

83

photographs. I'll bring a camera; you lick 'em, I'll snap 'em.
And then you slash their ball with a knife. That'll be a docu-
ment for you. Well? — the man got enthusiastic and leaned
forward and focused his eyes on the mist that separated
him from the players till he could no longer see them.

The old man had stopped listening; he turned away and
moved off with upraised head as though wanting to hear
the road before him; he stepped softly, placing his footsteps
with care, and was concealed by the wing of the dark
memorial, and by the mist.

— Well? Fancy a drop? — the man brightened up. And
how about those Jews? What? As you were saying. Fancy
a drop?

And he peered about, guarding on all sides, then pressed
his fingertips on his swollen eyelids and mumbled — An
eclipse, it's an eclipse, everything's dark, it's an . . .

World of Worlds

A monotonous dawn settles on the town and darkness slowly seeps back into the porous walls.

Outside the food store two tramps slept heavily on a broken park bench; sleep had dazed them the previous evening, before the shop closed, before they had emptied their beer bottles; since then they'd been clutching those bottles between stiffened hands, not spilling a drop; the light silvered their stubble.

White fluff drifted from the slender poplars and shrouded their heads, shoulders, thighs and knees, so that they looked like two down-at-heel angels; one of the angels shuffled his swollen feet along the paving stone; probably dreaming he was on the run...

A truck drew up alongside the curb, its motor died, and the driver's head collapsed onto the steering wheel; the glassy horn stirred the birds in the crowns of the poplars, but the sleepers on the park bench didn't budge.

A dour delivery man lowered the back hatch and pulled out crates of bottles that tinkled like Japanese bells and swung them into a pyramid, one on top of the other; when the tip of the pyramid began to lurch, he hitched a steel poker to the bottom crate, leaned forward like a bargehauler and struggled towards the glass door of the shop, till his flushed brow touched the pane; he rested quietly, then roused himself and returned to the van and heaved more crates, crashing them against the concrete as though to stifle his own pain.

— What an unholy racket those crates make — an unexpected voice came out of the darkness that still prevailed along the wall of the neighbouring house.

— What's the point of delivering so much soda water. When there's no food to be had, for love or... All that bloomin' soda stuff.

— We'll end up eating it.

— Or worse.

The man dragged his pyramid of crates toward the shop, pressed his forehead against the cool glass; then some gigantic insect scuttled out through a crack in the doorway, paused by the crates and twitched its long feelers.

— A cockroach, a cockroach — voices exclaimed.

— Kill it! Kill the cockroach!

— That's no cockroach. That's a grasshopper.

— Grasshopper my foot. That size? And black? It's a cockroach!

— It's not a cockroach! I knows a cockroach when I sees one. It's a grasshopper I tell you.

— Look at the size of it! A grasshopper'd be greenish-like.

— And it'ud hop — someone chipped in. — And this 'ere beastie don't hop. It just scuttles.

— Maybe it's had too much to eat...

— Too much to eat! When all they've delivered is soda water. Eaten too much soda water.

— Well then, drunk on soda water.

— You're drunk on soda water yerself, mister. That'll sure be a cockroach.

And the man withdrew his heated brow from the pane and without a word lifted the metal bar with which he'd been hauling the crate above his head, froze for a moment in that splendid gesture, then struck the insect with such gusto that sparks flew from the paving stone.

— Wow. Did 'im in with a poker. That cockroach I mean — a woman's voice piped up.

— Grasshopper. He'd have been scared to bash a cockroach.

— He missed anyway.

— Maybe he wanted to miss. He didn't have to, not unless he wanted to.

Two men were heading in the direction of these dull voices; they stopped to shake hands, then looked about — You going to the passport bureau too? — one of them asked. — Yeah, sure — and again they peered round — it can't be far from here — the darkness that concealed the building was slowly falling away to reveal a long line of people clinging to the ashen wall.

— Are you last? — one of the men asked.

— I don't know — the woman replied. I've got number hundred and twelve and I'm hanging on to it. At the front there's a social committee with a list. You have to sign on.

— Hundred and twelve — this early?

— Why, we've been here since one a.m. I've only just come along, so I'm hundred and twelve.

— Names, please! — startled by a voice from behind, they turned about, but it was only the committee chairman gripping a slim notebook tightly between his fingers, so they gave their names, and he wrote them in angular, technical calligraphy in the appropriate column and said — You're hundred and thirteen, hundred and fourteen; we check the list through every hour; anyone not here drops out; I'm going up to the front.

— Hundred and fourteen. That means standing here all day

— said the man.

— No, not quite, at the latest till midday — hundred and twelve replied, then fell silent.

— We'd better stick it out — the man said. — Because right now they appear to be granting passports. Maybe we could take it in turns.

— Oh, no — the woman interjected. — The number has to be confirmed personally. Otherwise, you're dropped from the list. Rules is rules.

They did not reply.

— The office doesn't open till eight — the woman volunteered. — A good couple of hours to go.

One of the men pulled out a packet of cigarettes.

— Beats our last meeting, eh?

— Yeah, how 'bout that mechanic who came along and poked about in the wires behind our bench, because they thought the bugging had broken down? We were just keeping quiet.

— And that taxi driver looking for his passenger who'd just dropped in but didn't come out again. He kept asking if there was any other exit, but the duty sergeant denied it. I was summoned again twice and I got to know the taxi driver. He kept popping in to enquire after his passenger and reckoning how much he'd clocked up on the meter to date. Till they were sick and tired of him. Six months later they admitted he'd been amnestied. And the taxi driver emigrated and returned to his profession. He's lecturing in mathematics at some university.

— The bugging was a good scene for a story. Did you write anything?

— No.

— Nor did I.

— Quite honestly I didn't know how. It's like that with everything now. I don't know what to write about. What's important. What will be important in the future. They're envious in the West that we have such an interesting country to write about. But I don't know what's so interesting about it. Or what's essential. It's misted over. Washed away. Like soap suds. And that is the essence of our times, of our epoch in general: grey froth. And everyone's writing memoirs now. Diaries. Publishing their notebooks. Everybody's escaping into the past. Publishing underground. Overground. A deluge of notebooks. Everyone's escaping into the past. No one is capable of taking on the present.

— On the one hand there's an indefinable, elusive greyness. On the other, myths. How does one fight a myth? Fight mythology? This country wallows neck-deep in it. Always has done. How does one tackle that? It was always premature to tackle it. One always had to wait for the myth to fade. Only it never did. Even stupidity can be sacrosanct in this country, the sacred cow of the cliché. One day maybe. Now it would mean sticking one's neck out. Everyone's bunking off into the past. So am I. Into my own private past. It's interesting. Meanwhile I'll try to get this passport, relishing the thought that I can either stay abroad or return to this country. Or else announce I'm staying and watch how many people who've already made that decision suddenly get the wind up. One more snout at the trough.

A young man sneaks up to the line outside the passport office, hugs the wall and hides his face in his shirt collar, observing the situation closely...

— Do you think there's any point? — he asks after a moment's acclimatization.

— Point in what?

— In my applying. Will they let me?

— Course they will. They're easy on passports now.

— But I'm fresh from military service.

— That I don't know. In that case you may have to wait a bit. I don't know.

— Mind you, I haven't done full service. Only a month. They had to discharge me, seeing I was getting schizo. All because I couldn't take the weight of military secrets. The responsibility. I didn't finish the course, handed in my gun. Is there any point?

— Point in what? — someone else got interested.

— In my applying. Have I got a chance?

— You're bound to. They're pretty easy now.

— But I'm fresh from the army. Though I handed in my gun.

— Now an acquaintance of mine when his son was born registered him as a daughter, so she, I mean he, wouldn't be called up. But truth will out: somebody squealed, and he didn't get a passport. The father I mean. As for the daughter, I mean the son, I can't say. There was quite a rumpus. Turned really nasty. In other words, with the military you can never tell. Sometimes they give, sometimes they don't. Just to keep you on the hop.

— Well, I'll be making tracks. If that's how things stand — and he pushed off, hugging the wall as though in search of a prop, then slipped round the corner of the house, casting one last backwards glance.

— Well, but what's going to happen to this country? — one of them began to brood. — What next? Will anything more happen to this country?

— For sure. There'll always be something interesting here. Not in our lifetime though. One day, yes. For the time being they'll sink us, they will. And we'll sink ourselves, until we're dead stuck. The rest of the world can do quite nicely without us. Only no one's prepared to believe that we're simply a nuisance. They just refuse to believe it. Things will start happening here again one day. One day. Luckily we won't be around by then. Everyone's fed up to the teeth with us. Left and right. And below. This country bounces about all over the map. Sometimes it's on the map, sometimes it's not. It vanishes in one place, then reappears in another. Round and round in circles. They're sick of us, and afraid. Or rather, apprehensive.

The inert hand of the man asleep on the bench twitched and the bottle instinctively crept up to his mouth; lips thrust forward, imbibed the poplar fluff that had settled in a ring of foam on the bottle-neck; the sleeper choked, but slightly shifted his position, caught his breath, and started yelping while asleep. . .

A woman dashed up to the line trying to control her panting — Folks — she said looking ahead — folks, do let me skip in here, eh?

— Whatever next. Barger! — and people laughingly shrugged their shoulders without even turning around. The committee chairman, convulsively clutching his slim notebook, emerged at the woman's side — Pull the other, it's got bells on — he said, tapping a lean finger on the green cover.

— But I'm an exception, I've been trying to get here for a week, because when they entered my number, the one that's coded in my passport, they got it wrong and keyed me in as a priest. Now they won't let me out of the country, so I'm stuck. You're down as a priest, they say, and a fine sort of priest you are, they say. You work that one out, then we can talk, they say.

— Priest or no priest — the committee chairman replied — That's no concern of mine. But this — he waved the school pad — is what we must abide by — and numerous heads nodded their approval.

— I'm fed up with interesting events by now — one of them said. — I just don't want to be part of it any more. I can't anyway, because I don't know how to write about these interesting events. And that's the only way I could participate. For years I could always find the key; it existed, it was ready. Now one has to write straight, and I can't write straight, because I'm made differently. My brain's Aesopic. And I can't shake off that language of allusion and the old forms, passé though they may be. I'm out of touch with my time. I don't speak the new language. Everything I try to do is impeccable, of course, only unfortunately it's dead. Propaganda. So I go round in circles locked up inside my own world, just like everybody else, and that's my space, just like everybody else. And so we go round in circles. No one wants to stick his neck out. We lack the tools. Make do with substitute forms. Play at waiting.

— Everyone's waiting for something — someone chipped in from the side; in an attempt to catch their words, he stooped forward with his head askew. — Everyone's waiting for something. Only we don't know what for — he said with a blissful smile.

The line stood waiting in drowsy silence. Nothing could move it now; only one woman was watching; she nodded her head and said to no one in particular, without soliciting support — Now my son, the rector in person hands him his coffee, yes; he's got a university diploma, an M.A. — she shook her head in astonishment and fell silent.

— So it's definitely handkerchiefs. Pocket handkerchiefs.
— Hankies, of course. An absolute must.
— And Chinese scarves. With fringe. Brilliant.
— Bed linen. Absolutely essential.

— But where to buy all those hankies? And Chinese scarves with fringe? And linen? Where are we s'posed to buy it all?

— There's just been a bulk delivery to our newsstand. It's so cluttered with bed linen there's no room for newspapers. It's quite handy too, 'cause it's open till ten. We can get it from the newsagent. People come and stock up on bed linen right into the night, since it's open till ten. They sneak past with sheets and stuff way after dark, I tell you.

— Crystals, of course. Irons.

— Irons are unobtainable.

— You're right. Must be organized.

— You say one thing, he says irons. Born yesterday, were you? Am I s'posed to teach you what's what? An old codger like you? Really!

— Fox furs, obviously. Fox furs.

— Ah yes, fox. Sure.

— Plastic jackets, pre-wrinkled.

— Lada spare parts. The lot. Anything we can lay our hands on. Every conceivable wheel valve.

— It all sells like hotcakes to the Soviets. Like proverbial hotcakes.

— Mind you, for Greece it's obviously mixers we want. Lots of mixers.

— All sorts of robots, kitchen gadgets too.

— Tools for Greek craftsmen. Every conceivable tool. Vices, bolts, nuts, screws. Whatever we can get.

— Tape recorders, portable TVs, fox furs.

— Lady, but you don't want foxes for the russkies. You've got it muddled.

— I said it was for Greece. Fox furs.

— For the russkies you mainly want electronic watches. Best of all with a bleep. There's not a russki can resist it.

— And Bulgaria. Gold belts, sunglasses, pendants, earrings. The more the better.

— Alarm clocks for Greece. Don't you dare forget alarm clocks for Greece. Lots of pyjamas. Balls.

— What sort of balls? Large? Small? Footballs or what?

— Any balls, big, small, what have you. They're crazy about 'em.

— If you're going to Greece, gas cylinders're the thing. Any amount. And water heaters, because they haven't heard of them, backward lot. Hair dryers.

— But where are we going to buy it all? The shops are empty. Where are we going to buy it all?

— Well, presumably not in the shops.

— You're coming back via Turkey, madam, right? So buy cotton there, right? So you bring the cotton into Poland, right? Then you're sitting pretty, right? And you start organizing your next trip. Because you're sitting pretty.

— I'd rather take electronic bleeper watches. I'm in the trade, they make money out of me, so why not. I'd recommend a lady's garter belt. I crammed up to three hundred and twenty pieces on one belt. That's my limit to date. This season I'll be using a bra too. They're mad on those bleeper watches. They'd gladly kill to have one.

— But where to buy all these marvels, eh?

— If you don't know that, lady, there's no point me talking to you.

— Only Greece. Only Greece.

— It would be my first trip abroad since the seventies — one of them said. — I'm terribly afraid of leaving, because I'm afraid of how things here will look from the other side. I don't mean terror, persecution, poverty, and the rest. What I'm most afraid of is that it may all seem sadly grotesque. Now it's all right to view the grotesquerie from over there. But when I return? How will I stand up to it then? Perhaps

94

the whole trip is senseless? Perhaps I'd better stick to what I'm used to?

— You haven't left yet. Steady on. You haven't left yet — the other one replied.

— Looking at it all I'm reminded of the negro Zmijewski.

— Who?

It was daylight by now, but the line strung along the wall outside the passport office was unobtrusive. Newcomers first had to get their bearings before walking up and giving their names to the committee chairman, who assigned them a number. They took up their position at the end and waited and watched awhile to become familiar with the group, get acclimatized and feel like a full-fledged member.

The sunlight smote the two angels asleep on the bench; one of them wanted to shield his eyes, made an uneasy, imprudent move and rolled over the gap in the bench bang onto the concrete sidewalk without spilling one drop from his bottle; the shadow from the metal bar bisected his face from forehead to chin giving the angel a pensive expression as he lay on the pavement; his mate asleep on the bench stretched out his hand and in a trance fumbled the bars by his side where his companion had been lying; his hand ceased moving, and he whimpered...

— I once wrote an article — one of them said. — Things were already getting stagnant, no one wanted or even knew how to write any more, and some of the minor clandestine papers were in real trouble finding authors; it was essential to start a polemic with that article, but no one felt willing or able to take issue with it, and in the end I had to write an attack on my own piece... With a few abusives for good measure in a letter to the editor...

— Viewed from one angle, it's getting to be more and more

like the story of the negro Zmijewski. I once even dreamed I was Zmijewski — the other one said.

— Who on earth is the negro Zmijewski? What happened to him?

— There was some sort of jamboree in Warsaw in 'fifty-five. Remember?

— Sure.

— Its exact name was the World Youth and Student Festival for Peace and Friendship.

— That's it.

— Well, there was this festival and the delegations flew back to their various corners of Poland and the world, and one girl delegate from Bialystok felt a bit off colour, so to speak. And nine months later all became clear, she gave birth to a black child. She was so involved in the festival, you see. The progressive black delegate was no longer to be identified, so the little negro boy was given his mother's name, Zmijewski, and grew up in Bialystok. He picked up the local dialect and even the singsong accent. Thereafter it was all predictable. He joined Solidarity, became a major activist in time, then martial law came. He may have been interned, I'm not sure. Let's assume he was. He came out and after a while he emigrated to the States, where he met other blacks and began to fraternize with them, as with his own kind. But when he tried to persuade them Reagan was the best president they could dream of, they cracked him one on the beak; it became a sort of habit, he proselytizing them for Reagan, they beating him up. And that's the story of negro Zmijewski. From Bialystok.

— The negro Zmijewski — the other one said in a reverie.

A small Fiat had drawn up outside the passport bureau; its windows were plastered with bright-coloured stickers in foreign languages, but the largest was in Polish, *I'm Castrol*

Your Loyal Oil; an extra wiper was mounted at the rear and a special plastic fin in front so the car held the road at high speed, also a radio aerial on a special spring and a towing hook shaped like a cat's head jutting out from the car's body...a man jumped out and looked round and saw the line; even as he walked toward it, his vitality ebbed and he shrivelled, hunched and became one among the many; a woman scrutinized the garish car, lost herself in thought, then said — If you ask me, things are the way they are because the whole government's festering with Jews...

— That's it — one of them said after a while. — In a church on the Vistula they're selling the *Protocols of the Elders of Zion*. Quite openly.

— In church, in church — the woman overheard them. — And you're one of those, aren't you now, that claims the country's anti-semitic? There's a lot of talk right now, there is. And you mean you don't know who's behind it all, eh? Whose interest it's in? You don't know? Eh?

— Do stop pestering — he said quietly, and with an effort.

— He's a fine one — the woman bridled. — He's a fine one, isn't he? — And she shrugged her shoulders. — Did you hear that? — She turned to her neighbour.

— We always helped them — the other woman assented. — Always. Always. It will all come out now, 'cause they've announced they're going to expose history's blank pages. I mean, when my dad saw them being transported to the camps, he felt awfully sorry for them, felt sick even. And he was a colonel. So there.

A clamour of voices rang out from the cross street, and round the corner a bearded elderly man wearing tight short trousers appeared, followed by a well-disciplined line of children in scout uniforms; they swayed in unison bearing aloft streamers, symbols and totems, and sang mechanically,

Though grey it is our colour, Our uniforms are grey, We're brave and bold at heart, And when we swoop upon our foe, He's taken off his guard.

The man in the short trousers looked round, saw he'd fallen out of step, marked time to catch the rhythm, and pressed forward on the wave of weary voices, *And I grab the wick and bottle, Pounce and throw it fast; If they shoot me for my country, I shall breathe my living last . . .*

The two feathered angels stirred, raised their eyelids on eyes like carnelians as a satiated sort of smile crept across their faces; both started to stand up as though to test their powers and drank in the words of the song; when the last scout had marched past brandishing the totem, both blew the white rings of poplar dust from the bottles and gulped and spat — Yes, yes — one of them mumbled — that's the way it ought to be, you'd better believe it, youth, youth — and they tottered behind the vanishing parade, overtook it and tried to fall into step. One shook his head the better to regain control — See how they go, that's the way to do it — and they clumsily tried to join in the song, like two guardian angels watching the troop . . .

— The negro Zmijewski? — one of them said.

— From Bialystok — the other replied.

— It's long past the hour — cautious voices murmured.
— It ought've opened a long time ago. It's the same everywhere. Anything to fray the nerves. Anything to harass.

— If it was nothing worse than that — someone reflected. It's all done with a view to putting us at odds. That's what the present policy is all about.

— But something must be done. They ought've started receiving applications half an hour ago . . .

— Tell the chairman to do something about it. He couldn't wait to be chairman, now let him do something . . .

— Chairman, chairman — the chairman was getting worked up. — When anything goes wrong it's always the chairman's fault.

He braced himself, raised his hand and tapped so delicately on the metal door that its plate did not respond.

The line froze in expectation, all ears. — Now you see —the chairman said softly — no sound or si...

He leaned helplessly against the door and hooked his elbow on the handle; as the door gave way slowly, the committee chairman at first stiffened, then retreated, as though choosing to mingle with the crowd...

The people stood still, but since no one appeared in the doorway, heads craned forward; the line began to pulsate gently — What's up, what's going on there, why's no one going in? — Those at the rear lost patience and pressed nearer the door; finally the chairman mustered up his courage, cleared his throat, straightened his shoulders, and led his troop to the back of the waiting room shielding himself with the sixteen-page school pad.

The line crammed its way chaotically in behind him until the surge halted and no one else could squeeze into the room; people inside no longer kept in sequence and those at the back again lost patience and pushed or marked time...

Those who had entered now stood silently hanging their heads, and the committee chairman turned to stone before them...they saw a steep corridor ahead clad in grey oil-painted panelling, and another alien line stretched as far as a grey door with a bulletin board and was pressing and pushing down that corridor, at the head of which stood another alien committee chairman clutching a slim school pad and entering something on a chart...

As the metal door shuddered halfway open, a woman's torso appeared; she bowed her retreat, paused and bowed again, holding on to the handle, then took another step backwards and was about to close the door, but she stuck her head once more through the narrow crack as though to give one last and final bow, but at the same time pulled the heavy door with all her might and . . .